# Ramsey's Praise

# Ramsey's Praise

## Vanessa Miller

Book 4
Praise Him Anyhow Series

Vanessa Miller
www.vanessamiller.com

Printed in the United States of America
© 2013 by Vanessa Miller

Praise Unlimited Enterprises
Charlotte, NC

Other Books by Vanessa Miller

How Sweet The Sound
Heirs of Rebellion
The Best of All
Better for Us
Her Good Thing
Long Time Coming
A Promise of Forever Love
A Love for Tomorrow
Yesterday's Promise
Forgotten
Forgiven
Forsaken
Rain for Christmas (Novella)
Through the Storm
Rain Storm
Latter Rain
Abundant Rain
Former Rain

Anthologies (Editor)
Keeping the Faith
Have A Little Faith
This Far by Faith

EBOOKS
Love Isn't Enough

A Mighty Love

The Blessed One (Blessed and Highly Favored series)

The Wild One (Blessed and Highly Favored Series)

The Preacher's Choice (Blessed and Highly Favored Series)

The Politician's Wife (Blessed and Highly Favored Series)

The Playboy's Redemption (Blessed and Highly Favored Series)

Tears Fall at Night (Praise Him Anyhow Series)

Joy Comes in the Morning (Praise Him Anyhow Series)

A Forever Kind of Love (Praise Him Anyhow Series)

Ramsey's Praise (Praise Him Anyhow Series)

Escape to Love (Praise Him Anyhow Series)

Praise For Christmas (Praise Him Anyhow Series)

His Love Walk (Praise Him Anyhow Series)

# 1

She was standing about six feet away from him, holding a beautiful bridal bouquet when Ramsey Thomas first took notice of her. Long flowing hair, olive skin tone, sparkling hazel colored eyes. The gown she wore showed off every bit of her shapely body. Ramsey was almost to the point of drooling when his brother Ronny nudged his shoulder and said, "Please tell me you're not drooling over the bride like that?"

Ramsey turned to his brother with furrowed eyebrows. The bride was Jewel Dawson and she was marrying his younger brother, Dontae Marshall. Ramsey was the best man so it would be a bit awkward if he was standing before God and a whole congregation of folks, lusting after the bride. "Shut up, idiot. I'm not drooling over Jewel," Ramsey whispered and then turned back around so he could continue taking in the lovely view of Maxine Dawson, Jewel's oldest sister and maid of honor.

A few months back Dontae had tried to hook him up with one of the Dawson sisters, but he'd been completely wrong about which one Ramsey would be interested in. Dawn, the middle sister, although just as beautiful as her other sisters, she was too short for him, and their personalities leaned more toward them becoming best of friends rather than having any kind of love connection. But Maxine Dawson was a woman that Ramsey would like to invest some time getting to know.

As if feeling his gaze on her, Maxine's eyes met Ramsey's just as the preacher said, "I now pronounce you man and wife." As Dontae took Jewel in his arms, Ramsey winked at Maxine. He grinned as her cheeks turned red from blushing.

Ramsey wanted to ask her on a date right then and there. But no matter how much Maxine was taking up space in his head, he wouldn't do anything to spoil this moment for his brother.

Later that evening while at the reception, Ramsey was standing with his father, Ramsey senior and his stepmother, Carmella when they started in on him. "I guess we'll be attending your wedding next, eh, son?"

Ramsey ignored his father and let his eyes span the room. He was looking for Maxine, but he'd never admit that to his father, and certainly not to Mama Carmella. If she knew he had his eye on a woman, she'd start praying and call down Elijah, Moses and a couple heavenly angels to get Ram to make a move. Ram was the nickname Carmella had given him. His family had taken to calling him that as a way of distinguishing between him and his father.

"Who's Renee talking to?" Carmella asked, pointing over by some tables in the back.

Ramsey's head swiveled back around. He had three sisters, Joy, Raven and Renee. And he was very protective of all of them. But he tended to watch out for Renee just a bit more. The girl made a career out of finding bad in a room full of good. Ramsey recognized the smooth talker Renee was grinning up at immediately. Marlin Jones was a high powered real-estate developer whom Ramsey had dealt with on occasion. He didn't like the way the man did business. There was something too slick about him. "I'll be back," Ramsey told his parents.

Carmella caught his arm. "Now Ram, don't you go over there bothering your sister. She is old enough to make her own decisions."

"I'm not going to do anything. I know the guy, so I just want to say hello." And goodbye, he added under his breath. As Ram pressed forward, Marlin put his hand on Renee's shoulder, her head fell back as she laughed ridiculously at something the man said. Marlin must have been telling Renee the funny one about how his tax returns were complete fiction and how the IRS was about to audit him for all of his wrongdoing.

"I like the way you laugh. I normally don't come to weddings, but I'm so glad I accepted this invitation," Marlin was saying as Ram advanced on them.

"And why is that?" Renee asked, beaming up at Marlin.

"Because I met the most beautiful girl in the whole state of North Carolina."

Ram wanted to throw up all over Marlin's playa rap. He only prayed that Renee could see through him. But just in case she couldn't, he was about to do some playa hating. Ram tapped Marlin on the shoulder, getting his attention. "Marlin, I didn't know you were attending my brother's wedding."

Swinging around, Marlin had to lift his head to address Ramsey, who was at least a half foot taller than he. "Hey Ramsey, I had no idea that Dontae was your brother. But my mom is best friends with Jewel's mom, so I had to come."

"Gotcha." Ramsey threw a look at Renee and then told Marlin, "Well it was nice seeing you. Do you mind if I have a word with my little sister?"

"I thought Charlotte was a big city. But look how small it's suddenly become. I cannot believe that this beautiful woman standing next to me is related to someone with a mug like yours," Marlin said lightheartedly.

"Believe it." Ram didn't know how much longer he could hold his fake smile in place, so he quickly put his arm around Renee and began walking away from Marlin. "See you later," Ram said while still smiling and waving.

"What are you up to, Ram?"

"I'm just trying to get you away from that guy."

With a quizzical expression on her face, Renee wanted to know, "Why in the world would you do something like that?" She pointed toward Marlin. "The guy is a dream...

successful, handsome. There's no bum stamp on his forehead."

"Yeah, but there ought to be a dog stamp on it," Ram replied back.

Rolling her eyes, Renee shoved her brother. "Don't start this stuff tonight, Ram. Just go back to the head table with the rest of the bridal party and stay out of my business."

Ram opened his mouth to protest, but Renee lifted her index finger and pointed toward his table. "Go, Ram. I'm not going to let you ruin my fun tonight."

He tried to help her. But if his sister wanted to be foolish and fall all over herself for a man who might be in prison in the next year or so, then she could have all the temporary fun she wanted. Ram turned toward the head table and saw Maxine seated next to his chair, eating a piece of wedding cake. So he took his sister's advice and set about minding his own business. He grabbed a piece of cake off the cake table and then took his seat. "Is this cake as good as you are making it look?"

Maxine picked up her napkin and wiped her mouth. "Did I look like I was starving?"

"You were getting it in, that's for sure."

"I deprived myself of all sweets for over a decade. Now that I don't have to worry about being rail thin anymore, I was probably a little too excited about eating this cake."

Ramsey picked up his napkin and wiped the white icing she'd missed from her chin. "Don't worry about it, cake looks good on you."

"I bet you say that to all the girls," Maxine joked as she took another bite of her cake.

Ramsey thought about the line he'd just heard Marlin running on his sister and he didn't want to come across like that. But if he was honest with himself, from the moment he saw her, he'd been mesmerized. He wanted to get to know this woman in the worst way and he wasn't trying to blow his opportunity by acting like a jerk. "I'm not trying to hand you a line. The plain truth is, I think you're beautiful and I would love to take you out some time."

Dontae, the groom and Ronny, the all around clown were standing behind them. Ramsey hadn't seen them until it was too late. After he told Maxine that he wanted to take her out, both Dontae and Ronny cupped their hand around their ear and said, "Say what?"

Okay, yeah, when Ramsey first came to the city and Dontae tried to hook him up with one of the Dawson sisters, he'd been adamantly against it. He hadn't wanted to be fixed up because he'd just gotten out of an awful relationship with a bipolar woman who made Glenn Close seem like a reasonable woman. So, he needed that hiatus. He turned to his brothers and said, "I'm gon' tell y'all like Renee just told me, get somewhere and mind your own business."

Ronny held his hands up. "We know when we're not wanted. And besides, we have better things to do than to watch you get shot down."

As his brothers walked off, Ramsey turned back to Maxine. "Excuse them. They don't know much about home training, outside training or any other kind of training, for that matter." A giggle escaped Maxine's beautiful lips. Ramsey saw an opening and took his shot. "See, I'm already making you laugh. Imagine how much fun the two of us would have on a date."

"I'm sure it would be wonderful." Maxine couldn't stop grinning. "It's just too bad that you didn't ask me out before I decided to become a mom."

Ramsey's eyes trailed downward and stopped at her mid-section. "I would have never guessed that you were pregnant. When are you due?"

"I'm not pregnant," she said matter-of-factly.

Ramsey took a bite of his cake, took a moment to chew it and then said, "Correct me if I'm wrong, but don't you need to be pregnant in order to become a mom?"

"I would love to have a husband before I become pregnant." Maxine shrugged. "But since my husband hasn't found me yet, I decided to adopt."

"A little impatient, aren't you?"

A tinge of regret dimmed Maxine's eyes as she said, "The truth is, I thought that I wanted nothing more than to be a model and once my modeling career was over, I intended to parlay that success into an acting career." She shrugged again. "But I can't act, I'm tired of modeling and since my biological clock is ticking like a time bomb, I decided to adopt."

Ramsey was a bit surprised that Maxine had shared so much with him, given the fact they didn't know each other well, but maybe she thought of him more like a brother, since her sister had just married his brother. He hoped to

God that she didn't think of him that way, because he sure wasn't seeing a relative when he looked at her. "You look so young. I'm sure you have plenty of time to wait for the right man to come along."

"Like they say, black don't crack," Maxine told him with a smile. "But seriously, I'll be thirty-four next year, so I don't have very many baby-making years left."

Ramsey shook his head at that news.

"What?" Maxine asked.

"It's nothing. I'm just amazed that a woman as beautiful as you hasn't found a man willing to make a baby with you."

"It's more difficult than you think. Most of the men I date are either insecure about my success or they think I'm too controlling."

"I don't know what kind of men you've been dating, but I don't mind releasing a little control every now and then. And I think your brand of success is very attractive."

That caught her off guard. She couldn't think of a quick comeback, so she simply thanked him for the compliment.

"Now, about that date..."

"You are kind of cute. And I bet we'd really enjoy ourselves on a date. But I've already signed up for diaper duty. Sorry." With that said, Maxine got up and walked away from Ramsey.

Ronny walked back over to the table, leaned over to his brother and said, "Struck out, huh? Should have asked me or Dontae. We could have told you that those Dawson sisters ain't no easy win."

\*\*\*

Ramsey was so tired when he arrived home that all he'd managed to do before falling into bed on top of his covers was take his jacket and tie off. Hearing Maxine talk about wanting to become a mother and being willing to adopt to make that happen, caused Ramsey to think about another woman who couldn't get rid of her child fast enough. He'd tried for over a year to get Brandi out of his head, but on a night like this his subconscious couldn't help but drag him kicking and screaming into that nightmare again.

Brandi was in his face yelling at him. Tears were rolling down her face as she kept demanding that he tell her why they couldn't work things out and be a family. Ramsey wanted to yell right back at her, "Because you're crazy." But she had torched his best suits the last time he'd informed her of the obvious. So he tried to reason with crazy, which was also probably a bad idea.

"Look Brandi, we gave it a go. But we aren't right for each other. You know that."

"Then what am I supposed to do with this?" Lightning fast, Brandi reached into her shirt and pulled out a baby. She was holding the child as if it was nothing more than a rag doll.

"Where'd you get that baby?" Ramsey was frantic, wondering who in their right mind would allow Brandi to watch their baby.

"She's ours, Ramsey. Our love child."

"Love didn't have nothing to do with it. And we do not have a baby."

The next thing Ramsey knew, he and Brandi were standing on the rooftop of his New York apartment and Brandi was holding the baby by its leg and threatening to throw it off the roof. "If you don't want me, then you don't deserve our child," she screamed.

"What are you doing, Brandi. Put that baby down."

"Say you love me, Ramsey. Say it!" The baby started crying.

Ramsey took a step toward Brandi. "You don't want to hurt that baby. Give her to me." He held out his hands.

Brandi stepped back; losing her footing, she began wobbling. Ramsey rushed over and helped to steady her. He then all but begged her to hand him the baby.

Brandi shook her head and ran away from him. "You'll never see this child again," she said just before jumping off the roof.

Screaming, Ramsey woke up in a cold sweat. Putting his hands to his face, Ramsey sat Indian style, trying to sort out what had just happened to him. "Lord, why can't I get that woman out of my head?"

\*\*\*

In another bedroom, about three hours away from Ramsey, Carmella Marshall was on her knees giving praise to God. He had done so much for her and seen her family through so many trials that Carmella didn't know what else to do but be grateful. Carmella was well aware that as long as they kept on living, somebody in her family was going to go through something that might just bring tears to her eyes, but she chose to praise God anyhow. Like the bible says, weeping may endure for a night, but Carmella had discovered that joy, does indeed, come in the morning.

Her children from her first marriage, Joy and Dontae had discovered the joy in praising the Lord along the road of recovering from their parents' crumbling marriage. And now Carmella had her sights set on Ramsey, Jr. He was the oldest of the seven grown children that she and her current husband were proud to be parents of. But Ram was dealing with something that he hadn't yet turned over to the Lord. So, once Carmella finished giving praise to her Savior, she turned her son over to the only One who could help him. "Lord, You see all and You know it all. Something is bothering Ram and he won't talk to me or his father about it. But I'm asking You to fix it for him. Give him peace and teach him how to lean on You. Amen and in Jesus' name I pray this prayer, believing that it is already done, so I give You praise for Your wondrous works."

"Amen," Ramsey, Sr. spoke up in agreement with his wife. He lifted the covers. "Now come to bed so we can get some sleep."

Carmella smiled at her sleepy husband and climbed into bed next to him. She had no problems falling to sleep that night because she knew that somewhere past the clouds in the sky, God had received her prayer and He was already working things out for Ram. She couldn't wait to shout the victory and do a praise dance over what God was about to do in Ram's life. She decided that she wouldn't wait, she was going to dance all up and down the church aisle on Sunday. Carmella wasn't one of those Christians who needed to see the promise before she believed.

"Whew. I praise You, Lord. Thank You for always blowing my mind with just how well You take care of us," she shouted through the room, before turning onto her side and falling to sleep.

# 2

One Year Later

It was almost midnight when Ronny and Dontae pulled into his driveway. Ramsey was dressed and waiting for them. How could he not be after the frantic call he'd received from Ronny, telling him that Renee had been rushed to Carolina Medical Center.

He jumped in the car and as Dontae sped off, Ramsey started firing questions at them. "Who called?" "What did she say?" "Is she all right?"

"Calm down, Ram, you know as much as we know at this point." Ronny rubbed his eyes and then looked at his brother. "Renee called me about twenty minutes ago. She told me that she was getting in an ambulance and going to the hospital."

"Did she say what happened?"

Dontae was gripping the wheel and driving like a New York cabbie, trying to hold onto a promised hundred dollar tip. "She didn't say what happened. And to tell you the truth, Renee sounded so scared and... and," he strained to get out the next part, "half dead, so we didn't want to keep her on the phone."

"Okay, let's just get there and figure it out," Ramsey said and he held onto the arm rest and let Dontae weave in and out of traffic. He and Ronny had both been crashing at Dontae's house when Ramsey first moved to Charlotte, but Ramsey had moved out just before Dontae's wedding. Since then Ronny had been crashing at Ramsey's place for a couple of months and then at Dontae's. Jewel didn't seem to mind because they all could see that Ronny was working towards something great. His new business venture was taking off. Ronny now had money in the bank and his credit situation was back on track.

Whenever Ronny was hanging out at Dontae's house, Ramsey sometimes felt left out. Like now. Why in the world did Renee call Ronny instead of him? He was, after all, the oldest brother and therefore Renee should have reached out to him since Dad was all the way in Raleigh. But ever since Renee had moved in with Marlin Jones, against everyone's wishes, she had been slowly separating herself from her family. Truth be told, Ramsey was even surprised that Renee had reached out to Ronny.

Dontae pulled up to the emergency room door, Ramsey and Ronny jumped out and rushed into the hospital and went straight to the information desk. "We're here for Renee Thomas. Can you tell us what room she's in?" Ramsey all but demanded.

"One moment, please." The receptionist clicked a few keys on her computer and then glanced back up at them. "She's being x-rayed right now." She pointed toward the waiting area. "Have a seat and we will call you back once she's in the room again."

"Okay, thanks." Ronny put a hand on Ramsey's shoulder as Dontae ran up to them.

"Did you find out anything?"

"She's in X-ray." Ramsey started walking towards the chairs in the waiting area. "Let's sit down."

For midnight on a Tuesday, the emergency room was full to bursting. But there were a couple of free chairs to the left of the double doors that led to the emergency room. Dontae and Ronny took those seats and Ramsey leaned against the wall. "Well, at least she's not in surgery," Ramsey said, trying to make himself feel better about the situation.

The double doors opened, a little boy ran out, pulling his mother with him. Head's swirled around, but they quickly turned away once they realized that Renee would not be walking through the door. "How long does an x-ray take?" Ronny asked.

The double doors opened again and a woman walked out carrying a small child. Dontae stood up. "Maxine," he called out. Maxine turned toward them. She smiled once she saw Dontae and then walked over to him. "Is Brielle sick?"

Maxine lovingly gazed at the little girl in her arms. "Her fever just broke. But she gave me quite a scare."

Ramsey hadn't seen Maxine since the wedding. She'd told him that she was becoming a mom and had no time for dating, so he'd tried to respect her wishes. But that hadn't stopped him from thinking about her, and dreaming about her beauty. Even at that late hour and with Maxine wearing a pair of jeans and plain white shirt, her beauty still took his breath away.

"So are you all here for Renee? I saw her back there," Maxine told them while adjusting the little girl on her hip.

Ramsey asked, "How's she doing?"

"Not too good from the looks of it. I just hope that whoever she was brawling with got it a whole lot worse."

Ronny shook his head, "She wasn't in a fight. Renee said something about an accident."

"Oh." Maxine backed off. "I guess I just assumed she'd been in a fight... Well, I hope she recovers soon."

As Maxine turned to leave, the little girl stretched her arms out and latched onto Ramsey's shirt. "Baba."

Maxine tried to unhook the child's hands, but she wouldn't let go. "Sorry, she's in a phase where she calls every man she sees baba. I think she's trying to say Daddy, but she can't get her fifteen-month-old mind off of her bottle long enough to make the distinction."

Ramsey took the little girl and held her. "Don't worry about it. What's her name, again?" Dontae had told him about the child, but he didn't remember the name.

"Brielle." At the sound of her name, Brielle lifted her eyes and looked from Maxine to Ramsey. Grinning, Ramsey looked down at the child in his arms. She was adorable. Ramsey found himself wondering how someone could have given this child away. There must be a heartbroken woman somewhere out there. Just like he was heartbroken over the child he almost had.

Maxine held out her hands to Brielle. "Come on, little one. Mommy needs to go home and get some sleep."

Ramsey pulled the child back into his arms and suggested, "I can walk you to the car if you'd like. It is after midnight... never know what kind of weirdos are lurking out there at this hour."

"Baba," Brielle said again.

Ronny laughed and then patted Ramsey on the shoulder. "Looks like you finally found a woman who actually wants to be with you."

"Ignore him," Ramsey said in a child-like voice as he talked to Brielle. "He wasn't raised right. But your mommy is going to make sure you are. Isn't that right, Brielle?"

Brielle giggled as Ramsey lightly pinched her cheek.

"Thanks, but I think we can manage." Maxine took Brielle out of Ramsey's arms and began walking way.

As Ramsey watched her leave, he noticed that Maxine was favoring her left side and had a slight limp. He caught up with her, took Brielle back into his arms, as if they were playing musical chairs with the child. "Come on, let me walk you to your car. Looks like you've injured yourself."

Maxine laughed, but accepted the help.

"What happened, did you fall and bruise your leg or something?"

"More like I bruised my ego." They arrived at the car, Ramsey looked as if he wanted to ask for clarification, but was unsure if he should pry, so Maxine went on and told him, "I tripped all over myself during a dance class. I actually entertained the idea of becoming a ballerina in my thirties. But tripping, falling and knocking some of the other dancers down on my way to the ground cured me of that aspiration."

Now it was Ramsey's turn to laugh. He loved the fact that Maxine was this beautiful, accomplished, well-traveled woman who could make fun of her own shortcomings. "I wish I had been there."

"No, trust me, you don't." She opened her car door.

Ramsey put the baby in her car seat, and began to miss her being in his arms the moment he let her go. "Does she get sick often?" he asked as he casually, leaned against Maxine's white convertible BMW.

Maxine shook her head. "Brielle is a wonderful baby... well; I guess I can't continue calling her a baby much longer. She'll be two in a few months."

"How long have you had her?"

"I adopted her thirteen months ago. We've been together ever since."

"I've never dated a mom before." Ramsey was staring at Maxine as if she was water and he had just pulled himself out of the Sahara desert. "But I don't mind if you don't mind."

Grinning at him, Maxine said, "I don't know, Ram. I'm still finding my way around this motherhood thing. And Brielle keeps me so busy I don't know when I could make the time for a date."

"It's simple, Maxine. You call a babysitter." Ram lifted himself from leaning on the car. Stepped a little closer to her, kept his voice low as he continued to inch forward. "Don't you think you deserve a little time to yourself?"

Looking down at her feet, she said, "It's complicated, Ram."

Ram wasn't about to let her get away with that. He put his index finger under her chin and lifted her head so that she was looking at him. "Let me uncomplicated it for you. I really like you, Maxine. I think we would be good together. So, what about you? How do you feel about me?"

Looking him in the eye, she didn't shy away from the subject at hand. "I don't know how good we would be together, but I'll admit that I find you attractive and enjoyable to be around."

"All this praise is giving me the big head."

Maxine playfully punched his shoulder. "You know what I mean."

He rubbed his shoulder as if he'd been hit by a heavy weight champ or something. "Yeah, I know what you mean... you're digging me."

"Okay, fine. I'm digging you. But I still have a child to think about."

"I'll tell you what. I'm going to give you a few days to fix all the complications and then I'll give you a call. How about that?"

To let them know that a third person needed to be considered in the conversation, Brielle started crying like something had jumped in the car and pinched her. "I've got to go. And you need to get back in the hospital. Renee really needs you."

Confused by that comment, Ramsey asked, "What do you mean by that? Did Renee say something to you back there?"

Maxine shook her head. "I can just tell that she's hurting, that's all."

Ram headed back into the hospital with Maxine's words weighing heavily on his mind. Something was telling him that the kind of hurt Maxine was referring to had nothing to do with the physical wounds Renee had incurred during whatever kind of accident she'd had.

As he was entering the hospital, the nurse had opened the double doors and was ushering his brother through. Ramsey rushed over to them and they were being escorted to his sister's room. "She's a little groggy from the pain medication so you won't be able to stay long."

"We'll keep that in mind," Dontae said.

"Is she going to be okay?" Ronny wanted to know.

"She's taken a few lumps, but she'll live." The nurse pulled the curtain back and then said, "I'll leave the rest for her to tell you all."

What rest? Ramsey wanted to ask, but he was too busy staring at his sister. She was laying on the bed with her back to them. Sling on her right arm. They could hear her crying as they approached. "We're here, Renee. Stop crying, hon. Do you need some more pain meds?" Ramsey kept talking as he walked around the bed. He stopped in his tracks as he caught sight of Renee's face. One of her eyes was swollen shut and purple. She had black and blue splotches on her face as if she had run repeatedly into an iron fist.

Ramsey rushed to her bed and put his hand on her side. Renee winced as Ramsey felt the bandage around her ribs. "Who did this to you?" he demanded.

"I fell." Renee's words were more of a mumble. And her face looked even more distorted as she tried to speak.

"I've seen ballers who looked better than you after having three hundred pound line backers pulled off of them. There's no way a simple fall did all of this to you." Dontae's nostrils flexed in anger.

Ramsey, Ronny and Dontae gave each other the look that said they knew exactly what had happened to their sister.

"I already told Ronny that I fell."

"Yeah, but fell into what or who is what we want to know," Ronny said as he stepped forward.

"The stairs, Ronny." Renee was still crying, but she was sticking to her story.

The nurse came into the room. She took Renee's blood pressure. Dontae pointed at his sister and asked the nurse, "What happened to her?"

The nurse shook her head. "We don't know. She won't say."

"What does it matter? I lost the baby," Renee sobbed, "I lost the baby."

"What baby?" Ramsey looked at his brothers, trying to determine if he was the only one surprised by what his sister had just uttered.

# 3

"I'm going to kill him," Ramsey declared after they left the hospital. "He beat that baby out of her on purpose."

"That would make him a monster... I can't believe that Marlin is like that," Ronny said.

"Is that because Marlin is investing in your business or can you honestly look us in the face and tell us that you believe Renee fell down some stairs as she claimed?"

"I sure don't believe it," Dontae interjected.

"Look, I'm as angry as the both of you, but I don't want to accuse someone of trying to kick a baby out of our sister's stomach before we have proof," Ronny said.

"Well you wait on the proof. We're going to Marlin's house to kick his guts out of his stomach and up through his throat," Ramsey said while Dontae sped out of the hospital parking lot and kept moving towards their destination.

Ramsey had been so furious with Renee for moving in with Marlin six months ago, that he rarely went to their house to check on her. Now he was wondering how many beatings his sister had taken since she started sleeping with the enemy. "We just left her with that monster. How could we do that? We knew it wasn't right for them to be living together like that." Ramsey was beside himself with grief. He was supposed to protect his sisters. How had he let something like this happen?

"Mama tried talking to Renee," Dontae offered. "But Renee wouldn't change her mind. She told Mama that God couldn't care less about whether or not she shacked up before getting married."

"We all know that's not true," Ronny said.

"I'll admit that I tried it once, when I was living in New York." Ramsey shook his head as memories of that nightmare situation tried to cloud his head. "It was the biggest mistake of my life. I'm a firm believer now. I can guarantee you that I'll marry the next woman I live with and I'll make sure I know everything about her background and mental health issues."

"Who was this crazy woman you were shacking up with? You've made reference to this woman before, but you've never told us her name." Ronny asked.

"I don't like to think about her, Ronny. Let's just concentrate on one nightmare at a time, okay?"

Dontae pulled into Marlin's driveway. The brothers jumped out of the car the moment it was put in park and began banging on Marlin's front door. When no one answered, Ramsey went around the back and checked a couple of windows; they were locked. He then checked the sliding door of the deck. It was as if all the angels in heaven were cheering him on as he opened the door.

"Marlin, where are you?" Ramsey yelled through the house. He didn't receive an answer back, but Ramsey smelled a rat, so he knew with everything in him, that Marlin was there, he just had to find him. "I'm coming for you, and I guarantee you that this house isn't big enough to hide you from me."

Ramsey searched throughout the house and finally found Marlin hiding in a closet in the master bedroom. Without asking any questions he dragged him out of the closet and punched him.

"She's lying. I never laid a hand on her," Marlin said while trying to keep himself from falling.

"Her face doesn't lie," Ramsey punched him again. By the time Dontae and Ronny ran into the room, Ramsey was pummeling Marlin.

They pulled him off of Marlin. Dontae said, "Calm down, Ramsey, I think he got the message."

But Ramsey reached out and touched Marlin again with a right hook. "He beat Renee, even knowing that she was pregnant. And for that I could kill him with my bare hands."

"If you hit him anymore, you just might kill him," Ronny said.

"I don't care." Ramsey was too enraged to think straight. "He's an animal and he needs to be put to sleep."

Marlin wiped his bloody nose with the sleeve of his shirt. "Your brother's crazy. He broke in my house. I'm calling the police."

"You do that and I'll make sure that Renee files charges against you," Ronny told him.

Dontae grabbed Ramsey's arm. "Come on, Ram. We've overstayed our welcome here. We might not get another invite."

"Now that Renee is out of here, I have no reason to come back to this house."

"She'll be back. Renee belongs with me. And I'm not letting her go."

Ramsey lunged at Marlin again, but Dontae and Ronny pulled him back. Ronny then told Marlin, "She's already gone. You'll never see her again." The brothers pulled out two suitcases from the walk-in closet and started pulling Renee's clothes off the hangers and grabbing her things out of the drawers.

From his spot on the floor, Marlin yelled back, "You can forget about me investing in your silly little business."

"No," Ronny declared, as he walked back over to Marlin and pushed his head back to the floor, "You can forget about me allowing you to invest in my business."

"You tell him, bro," Dontae said as the three brothers left the house with as many of Renee's clothes as they could carry.

***

Two days later Ramsey was on Interstate 85 taking Renee to their parents' house in Raleigh. Renee cried a lot during the three hour drive. She didn't talk much except to say, "I should have listened to you. I'm so sorry that I didn't."

His sister was bruised and bandaged and her arm was still in a sling, so he didn't want to be one of those gloating, "I told you so" kind of brothers. Ramsey lightly put his hand on Renee's shoulder. Trying to reassure her that brighter days were ahead, he told her, "This too shall pass, li'l sis."

"Don't be nice to me, Ramsey. I blew you off for an entire year because I wanted to be with Marlin. I was terrible to you, so it's just going to make me feel worse if you're nice about everything now."

"Well then you're just going to have to feel worse, because I'm not about to throw salt in your wounds. I love you, Renee. And I just want the best for you. That was the only reason I was against you getting involved with Marlin. And I certainly didn't want him moving you in without him putting a ring on your finger."

Rolling her eyes, Renee said, "Not you, too."

Ramsey kept his eyes on the road and hands on the steering wheel as he probed, "Not me too, what?"

"Daddy and Carmella got on my case when I decided to move in with Marlin. She and Daddy started talking about God's perfect plan for my life and all that mumbo jumbo. Carmella took it to another level, though, because she grabbed my hands and starting praying for me."

Ramsey really didn't understand his sister sometimes. She attended church on Sundays, but it didn't seem as if she was listening to the preacher. Come to think of it, he had no clue of what church she'd been attending in the last year. "Tell me something... have you been attending church since you moved in with that creep?"

"Marlin doesn't believe in organized religion." She shrugged. "To tell you the truth, I'm not so sure if I do either."

Ramsey wanted to jump all over that. Their family was full of bible believing church goers. He'd had his years of absence from the church, but he'd always known that God was real and that He was worthy to be served. How could Renee not believe? But he could feel the Holy Spirit guiding him... *it's not time yet.*

Leaning back against the headrest, Renee blurted out, "I wish I'd never met him."

Even though she hadn't said his name, Ramsey was positive that Renee was talking about Marlin. The pain in her voice was so consuming that Ramsey wished he'd gone back to that house and beat on that loser some more. But in truth, Ramsey knew that he still needed to repent to God for his actions. However, he couldn't lie to God and pretend to be sorry for what he'd done to Marlin, because he was nowhere near being repentant over that situation.

"You didn't tell Dad that I was pregnant, did you?"

Ramsey gave Renee a sideways glance. Fear was in her eyes. Little Miss I-can-do-whatever-I-want was actually worried about something after all. "No, I didn't tell him. I think you should be the one to tell him that, don't you?"

Renee didn't respond. She turned her head toward the window and let the tears fall down her cheeks as she thought about the baby that she had loved and lost way too soon.

Ramsey felt his sister's pain on that one. When he'd broken it off with Brandi, he hadn't known that she had been pregnant. But Brandi was so spiteful that she'd called him a week later and told him that the night he'd asked her to leave, was the night she was going to tell him that she was pregnant. She then told him that he didn't have to worry about child support, because she'd aborted their baby. Ramsey still had nightmares over what Brandi had done, feeling as if his actions had caused the death of his child.

He loved his career in the banking industry. He was good with numbers and had been promoted to vice president. But none of that was enough to keep him in New York, not after he'd discovered that his carelessness had cost him a child. It was Ramsey's cross to bear, but it was also the reason he had decided to try it God's way. No sex before marriage, that way he could guarantee there would be no babies by random off-their-meds women.

They pulled up at the house and got out of the car. Renee walked slowly. She was still in pain, but Ramsey figured that she was also in no rush to face their parents. He pulled her suitcases out of the trunk and then rang the doorbell.

Carmella swung open the door and ushered Renee and Ramsey into the house. "You poor dear. I have been sick with worry ever since Ram called."

"Thanks for letting me stay with you for a little while."

"Hush with all that. As long as Ramsey and I have a home, you and any of our other children have a home to come to in your time of need." Renee got this pained look on her face, so Carmella said, "I've got a pillow and a blanket on the couch in the family room. You go on in there and I'll grab something for you to eat and some pain pills."

Ramsey helped Renee lay down on the couch and then he went into the kitchen with Carmella. "Where's Dad?"

"He's at the gym, but he'll be here shortly." Carmella put a TV tray on the counter and then put on a bowl of soup, crackers and then poured lemonade into a tall glass. "I don't know how to thank you for bringing her home, Ram."

"Honestly, I didn't know what else to do. I didn't want her staying in Charlotte with Marlin still living there. So, I'm just praying that he won't come here looking for her."

"If he does, your dad will probably give him some more of what you already gave him," Carmella said as she placed a bottle of pain killers on the tray.

"So you heard about that, huh?" Ram had a sheepish grin on his face as he sat down behind the counter.

She gave him the eye. "You know God's word says to be angry, but don't let the sun go down on your wrath."

"I didn't, Mama Carmella. I went right over to Marlin's house as soon as we left the hospital. And trust me, I slept good that night."

She laughed. "I let my anger get the best of me a time or two in my life also. But God knows when we've taken more than we can bear. So, I'm not going to beat you up too much about what you did. I just hope we won't have to bail you out of jail before this is all over." She kissed Ram on the forehead and then headed into the family room with Renee.

Ram stayed at the house with his parents and Renee overnight. The next day he went to church with them while Renee stayed home. He then got on the highway and headed back home, hoping and praying that Renee would get the help she needed to mend. He also prayed that she would find a good man to marry and start a family with.

Two hours into his drive, he pulled off the highway to get some gas. When he got back in the car and was about to put the key into the ignition, his phone beeped, letting him know that an email had just come in. It was a Praise Alert from Mama Carmella. She used to send alerts out every week, but they had always been about how other people gave praise to God for doing this or that in their lives. Her praise alerts weren't as frequent these days, but they were personal.

This one was about Renee. Carmella was giving thanks to God and praising Him for bringing her baby girl back home. She even went so far as to praise God for healing Renee's wounds. That was the part of the alert that confused Ramsey.

He understood about praising God for the great and mighty things He'd done in our lives. But how could anyone praise God for something He hadn't done yet? It just didn't make sense to the natural part of his brain that said people get paid for performance, for what they do right in the moment, not what they will or might do in the future. So naturally, he had always thought that praises to God should be reserved for when He'd actually done something. But if God was able to get Renee through this awful time in her life, he wasn't about to question how and why it happened.

As he thought about Renee moving forward from this tragedy and someday starting a family with a man who was worthy of her, his mind drifted to Maxine and how beautiful motherhood looked on her. She hadn't slept around, become pregnant and then aborted the baby the moment it became inconvenient. She was wearing motherhood with pride and he had great respect for her because of that.

It was time for him to make contact with Maxine to see if she was ready to make room for him in her life. He'd forgotten to get her number that night at the hospital, but Dontae was on speed dial on his cell phone, so he hit the number 3 and waited for his brother to pick up the phone.

"How'd it go?" Dontae asked when he picked up the phone.

"Not bad. Renee seems resigned to dealing with her situation, and I really think she wants to be home right now. But that's not why I'm calling."

"What's up?" Dontae asked.

"Can you give me Maxine's telephone number?"

"I thought you already had it."

"No. She never gave it to me. But I wanted to check on her and her daughter."

"I'm not sure if Maxine wants me passing her number around to any and everybody who asks. You might be one of those types that like to stalk celebrities, for all I know." Dontae could barely keep the laughter out of his voice as he joked with his brother.

"Boy, shut up and give me that number."

"All right. Being a single mother, she might not have as many offers for dates these days, so she just might have lowered her standards by now," Dontae said just before giving out the number.

"Thanks for nothing, bro. Oh, and tell Jewel I feel sorry that she has to stay married to a bum like you."

# 4

Ramsey was thirty minutes from Charlotte when he punched in Maxine's number. She picked up the phone on the first ring and screamed at him. "Don't you call here again! Leave me alone."

Before Ramsey could respond, he found himself listening to a dial tone. "What in the world just happened?" Ramsey asked himself. Maxine hadn't been expecting to hear from him. But he doubted she would be so rude just because he got her number from Dontae without asking her if it was okay. He punched in her number again. And before she started yelling at him again, Ramsey yelled out to her. "This is Ram, what's going on over there?"

"Oh my God, Ramsey, I'm so glad you called." Maxine sounded frantic "My lights have gone out and someone is playing on my phone."

Taking charge, Ramsey told her," Make sure all the doors and windows are locked. I'm on my way." He took down her address and then kept her on the phone while he sped down the highway, talking to her by way of the

Bluetooth connection in his car so that he could keep both hands on the steering wheel. Because he was driving so fast, he needed a firm hold on the wheel.

When he arrived at the house, Maxine ran down the stairs, swung open the door and then threw her arms around him. "Thank you. I don't know what I would have done if you hadn't called when you did."

As Maxine clung to him, he got lost in the smell of lilacs and roses. He found himself wondering what her favorite perfume and shampoo were. He held her tighter, forgetting his purpose for coming until he heard the baby cry. Ramsey immediately released her, stepped back and said, "Where is the breaker box?"

"In the garage." She pointed him in the right direction.

"Okay, do you have a flashlight?"

"No batteries."

Ramsey went back to his car, popped the trunk, shuffled through the contents and came up with his flashlight. He rushed back to the house. "I've got mine, so you go check on the baby and I'll try to get your lights back on."

By the time Maxine made it back upstairs and lifted Brielle into her arms, the hall light came back on. She breathed a sigh of relief and headed back downstairs. Ramsey exited the garage and closed the door behind him. "That should do it."

"Thank you." Looking a little embarrassed, Maxine said, "I guess I should have known to check the breaker box, but to tell you the truth, this is my first house. I moved here from New York. And in the building I was living in, the super handled everything for us."

"Your sister told me you had been living in New York. I'm just surprised that I never ran into you."

Maxine chuckled. "Yeah, that was the strange thing about New York. There were times when I would run into people I knew all the time. But then I could go months without seeing any of my friends."

"That was one of the reasons I asked to be transferred to Charlotte. I needed to live in reality, rather than the alternate universe that is New York."

"I actually loved most everything about New York except for how big it is," Maxine agreed. They stood in the hallway, staring at each other for a long uncomfortable moment, then Maxine said, "Um, I made a cake just before the lights went out. I didn't get a chance to frost it, but if you'd like a piece I can put the icing on it quick enough."

Ramsey would do anything to prolong his stay with Maxine. If she wanted him to eat cake, that was all the better as far as he was concerned. His stepmom owned a pastry shop and Ramsey made his way there every time he went home, not to mention all the cookies and pies that she brought home with her. Ramsey rubbed his hands together. "Sounds good. What kind of cake did you make?"

"Carrot," Maxine told him with pride.

One of his favorites. Ramsey couldn't wait. Beautiful and could cook, too. He didn't know why God decided to smile down on him, but Ramsey sure wasn't about to try to act all humble and tell God he wasn't worthy... he was just going to accept the gift and keep his mouth shut.

Maxine was about to put Brielle in her high chair when she reached out for Ramsey just as she had done at the hospital a few nights ago. "No Brielle, just sit here while I put icing on the cake."

"Baba, baba," she said as she kept reaching for Ramsey.

"Let me take her. She can sit on my lap, if you don't mind." Ramsey sat down at the kitchen table and put Brielle in his lap. The child bounced around on his knee as she squealed with joy. "I think she really likes me."

"Yeah well, she better not end up being boy crazy as a teenager, or I'll have to home school her and lock her in the house until she goes off to college."

While watching Maxine frost the cake, Ramsey figured he'd get as much information out of her as he could before she threw him out for the night. "So, you really enjoyed New York, huh? Did you ever attend any Broadway shows?"

"I not only attended Broadway shows, I acted in a couple of them." She shrugged. "If you could call it acting."

"What do you mean?"

Maxine cut three pieces of cake, put two pieces on one saucer with a fork and handed it to Ramsey for him and Brielle. "One of the reviewers said, and I quote," She made like she was opening a newspaper to read from it. 'Maxine Dawson displays better acting skills while lying on a beach in a swimsuit being photographed. To be blunt, this is one model who shouldn't quit her day job.'"

"Just one reviewer's opinion," Ramsey said, trying to sound supportive.

"And the producer's, and the director's, and the other actors and the audience, and..."

"Okay, I get the picture. You really stunk up the place." Ramsey tried his best not to laugh in her face, so he pressed on. "Is that the reason you decided to move back home?"

Maxine sat down across from Ramsey and Brielle. "Actually, as I was getting older, my relationship with God was also growing. And suddenly it just wasn't as important to me to be this triple threat I'd always imagined myself being."

Ramsey started counting off, "Model," he lifted one finger, "Actress," he lifted another finger. As he lifted the third finger he gave Maxine a curious glance.

"Singer. My third talent was supposed to be singing," she confessed.

Brielle took a bite of the carrot cake, Ramsey fed her, but she spit it out and started crying. Ramsey glanced at the baby and wondered why she was crying as if someone had taken the cake away from her, when the cake was right in front of her.

Looking dejected, Maxine said, "She won't eat the baby food I made for her either. I try to make things healthier for her, but she's just not going for it."

Ramsey put a piece of the cake in his mouth and wanted to cry himself. It wasn't that Brielle didn't like healthier options; she probably just preferred food that actually tasted good. He would have spit it out if he didn't really, really want to take this woman out. Well, at least she didn't say that her cooking skills were her third talent; if she had, Ramsey would have to say that she was a threat all right. He put his fork down and pushed his plate aside.

"You don't like it either, do you?"

How could he tell this beautiful woman, whom he definitely had feelings for, that he hated her cooking. Ramsey wasn't that brave. "My stepmom bakes her carrot cake a little differently. I think I'm just used to the way she fixes it." He didn't care what he had to say; there was no way he was taking another bite of that cake. And apparently, Brielle wasn't going for it either. As tears poured down the child's face, Ramsey rubbed her back. "Stop crying, sweetheart."

Maxine picked Brielle up and began soothing the child by humming to her. Brielle stopped crying and laid her head on Maxine's chest. "There, there, my sweet little one."

"You've got the touch, evidently." Ramsey pointed at the baby. "She's gone to sleep."

Looking down, Maxine smiled. "It normally doesn't take long when she's tired. Let me go lay her down and then I'll be back to see you out."

The moment Maxine left the kitchen Ramsey rushed over to the sink, grabbed a glass out of the cabinet and immediately began rinsing the awful cardboard taste of that cake out of his mouth. Maxine was beautiful, but an Iron Chef she was not. He heard her coming back down the stairs so he went back to his seat and pretended that he'd been sitting there waiting for her all along.

As Maxine re-entered the kitchen, she set her iPad on the counter, turned it on and then pressed one of the icons. And just like that she had full view of Brielle's room. When she noticed Ramsey checking her monitoring system out, she said, "I like to make sure she's okay."

"That's pretty slick. That way you don't even have to get out of bed to check on her. Just turn on your iPad and it's like you're in the room with her."

"Not only that, but watch this." Maxine tapped on her iPad a couple of times and then turned the device towards Ramsey."

"That's us?" He waved his arms around enjoying seeing them togethers on camera.

"I have the monitoring system in about four rooms. If I ever have to leave Brielle with a babysitter, I want to be able to check in on her, no matter where she is in the house."

"That's probably the best way to do it. You never know what's going on behind closed doors these days."

Maxine lifted her iPad. "With this baby, I know a whole lot of what's going on in here."

"That's what peace of mind looks like."

Maxine set the iPad back on the counter and then all of a sudden she got this look in her eyes as if she'd just remembered something important. She snapped her fingers and said, "Eggs."

"What?" Ramsey's eyebrows went up as he questioned her one word sentence.

Popping her forehead with the palm of her hand, she told him, "I forgot to put eggs in the cake."

"I think you forgot the sugar, too," Ram told her as politely as he could.

Laughing, Maxine sat down across from him. "I used a red beet as a substitute for sugar." She playfully smacked his arm. "Some of the models back in New York used to do that when they needed a sugar fix."

Ram protested. "Hey, don't abuse me simply because I can't tell the difference between no sugar and the use of a beet for sugar. When it comes to my cakes and my women, I might add... I want all the sugar I can handle."

"Okay, so the next time I bake a cake for you, I'll make sure to put regular sugar in it."

"That's all I'm asking. And please don't forget the eggs." Glancing at his watch, he stood and pushed in his chair. "When might that be?"

"When might what be?" Maxine asked as she stood with him.

"You said you're going to fix me another cake." Lord knows he didn't want to suffer through another cake episode, but if it was the only way he could see Maxine again, he'd just put the hospital on notice that he might be coming in to get his stomach pumped.

The look on her face said she wished she could, but she opened her mouth and said, "Ram, I'm sorry but this week is going to be busy for me. Brielle and I just might be eating out a few days this week."

"I understand if you're busy, don't worry about it." Ram put his hands in his pocket and headed for the front door.

Maxine put a hand on his shoulder, Ram turned back around to face her. "Don't look so dejected. I'm not turning you down. I really would like to go out with you. But I'm rehearsing for my solo at church this Sunday. This is really important to me, Ram. I need to know if I can sing well enough to sing gospel music professionally. A producer has already offered me a contract. But I don't want to take it if I'm just going to get more bad reviews."

Smiling now, Ram said, "Don't you attend Dontae and Jewel's church?"

"Sure do."

"How about I come to church and cheer you on next Sunday. Then I can take you and Brielle out to dinner or whatever you want."

"Deal." Ram and Maxine shook hands on it. Then he said, "But you better be really cheering. You and Brielle hurt my feelings enough tonight with the way y'all refused to finish my cake."

Lifting one finger he reminded her, "A cake with no eggs and no sugar."

"Okay, but just help me out at church, all right?"

At least he didn't have to eat her cooking. "I'll be the one praise dancing down the aisle as you give glory to God with your voice."

# 5

Ram hated missing service at his own church, not to mention that he had to drive forty-five minutes to get to the University area where his brother's church was at. But if things went the way Ram wanted, he wouldn't have to do this for long. Because if he and Maxine hit if off the way he'd believed they would from the moment he watched her walk down the aisle at Dontae and Jewel's wedding, then his family might just be attending another wedding and Maxine would hopefully switch membership to his church.

Ram had to laugh at himself. *Pump your brakes.* He and Maxine hadn't even been on their first date yet and he was already singing the here-comes-the-bride song. The thoughts in his head made him pause for a second. He sat down on his bed and lowered his head. He needed to pray about this... ask the Lord if Maxine was the one or if he needed to look for another. After he finished praying, he waited for a moment to see if he was going to hear from the Lord. Sometimes he received answers to his prayers right away, other times he had to wait awhile. This was one of those wait-a-while times, so he grabbed his keys and headed out the door.

But Ram was just happy to even be having thoughts of love and marriage. He'd never met a woman that he'd fantasized about marrying. The closest he came to commitment was when he'd made the biggest mistake of his life and moved Brandi into his house. Ram had cared about Brandi, but it hadn't blossomed into full blown love. Yet and still, Ram wished he could turn back the hands of time and eat every syllable he'd spit out of his mouth the day he'd told Brandi that it just wasn't working out between them. If he had just waited one more day, then he would have known about the baby. Maybe he could have talked her into letting him raise his child, rather than aborting it.

This time, though, he was determined not to let things get that far with Maxine. Not unless he had a ring on her finger and had already said "I do".

Praise and worship was just about to get started when Ram arrived at the church. Dontae and Jewel had saved him a seat, so he squeezed in with them. "Thank you for coming to support Maxine. She's kind of nervous about the song she's going to lead. She'll be happy to have your support."

"I thought she was doing a solo." Ram said.

Jewel got a strange look on her face as she told him, "They made some adjustments to the song during rehearsals."

The praise and worship team was the best that Ram had ever heard. There were only four women and one man singing praises to God, but they sounded as beautiful as a large choir. Ram was on his feet praising like nobody's business, when he reminded himself that he needed to save some of it for when Maxine started singing. Wouldn't do to be all tuckered out by the time she got to the microphone. But then they began singing a slow praise song and he stopped dancing and just raised his hands in praise.

After offering, the choir stood and it was time for Maxine's big moment. The choir began singing Take Me to the King. The song started off really good and Ramsey stood up and began clapping just as he promised he would do. But then something went wrong. Maxine's voice cracked on every other word. Ramsey never lost his beat and he kept the smile on his face until Maxine handed the microphone off to another singer to finish the song.

Ramsey sat down, wondering what he was going to say to Maxine. She was certainly no Tamela Mann, the original singer of that song. But even though Maxine stunk up the place with her rendition of that song, she looked beautiful doing it. Ramsey decided that he would tell her how beautiful she was and how God loves to hear praise from his children. But he knew Maxine, and those lame responses weren't going to work with her... but it was all he had.

Ramsey was so intrigued by Maxine that he hardly heard a word the pastor preached that day. Maxine had so much to be proud of. She'd spent over a decade as a super model and been paid very well, if the house she was living in was any indication. But for some reason, she didn't seem content with all she had accomplished and was determined to discover something else she could do with the rest of her life. Ramsey just didn't understand why she didn't concentrate her efforts on doing something in the fashion industry since she already knew so much about it.

***

Maxine wished she could just grab Brielle out of the nursery and escape out of the back door of the church. She had almost called Ram last night to tell him not to come to church today. But she knew he would think she was just blowing him off. And there was no way she was going to make a man as kind and as fine as Ramsey Thomas, Jr. wait another second. It had been over a year since she'd told Ram that she couldn't get involved with him because she was going to become a mother.

She'd thought that her decision to adopt Brielle left her zero chance with Ram, but he seemed not to care about her single motherhood status. And Brielle was certainly over the moon about him. Her daughter was starting out young, but she already knew a handsome man when she saw one. Maxine had learned a long time ago that going just on looks was a sure fire way of ending up in a relationship with someone who was nice to look at, but had no substance, and no moral base... as far as Maxine could see, Ram was a very moral man... full of enough substance and character to go around.

She had made a mess of it today, though. He must have thought she was crazy or something. Maxine walked into the nursery, signed Brielle out and tried her best not to look anyone in the eye. But as she grabbed Brielle's hand and began walking out of the nursery, Sister Fowler stopped her and said, "You look like you need a hug."

How did she know? Sis Fowler worked in the nursery with the kids. Had she come into the hall while Maxine was howling at the moon rather than actually singing? Sis Fowler wrapped her arms around her and said, "You have a good voice, just need a bit more practice, that's all. So, don't let it get you down."

Well, guess that answered her question. Maxine smiled and walked away. Sister Fowler was simply trying to encourage her; she didn't realize that she had just crushed her spirit a little bit more. The people in her life thought Maxine was living on easy street and had no problems because of how much money she had earned in the fashion industry. But Maxine's modeling career was over and she was only thirty-three, with no desire to live a life of leisure, traveling the world doing nothing but discovering new places to shop. She needed to figure out what she was going to do with the rest of her life. She wanted to be a mother and have a career, but sometimes she wondered if she was just being selfish again. Maxine didn't like to think about how much selfishly pursuing her modeling career had cost her. She'd rather go face Jewel, Dontae and even Ram than dwell on those hateful memories. So she picked Brielle up and made her way back to the sanctuary.

"Hey girl," Jewel said as Maxine approached. "We waited for you. Thought we would walk out to the car with you."

"I don't need a bodyguard, but thanks for the thought, sis." Maxine kissed her sister on the cheek.

"We just wanted to be here for you," Dontae told her, with an uncomfortable look on his face. "I mean... with it being the first time you sang in front of a crowd and all."

Jewel poked her husband and tried to whisper, "You didn't have to mention the song."

"It's okay, Jewel. I know that I messed the song up. Sister Fowler already gave me a hug and some words of encouragement."

"I was supposed to be here for the encouragement," Ram reminded her. "I hope you didn't let someone else steal my job."

Maxine turned towards Ram and smiled. At least he was still there and hadn't left because it would be too awkward to face her. She'd once brought a date to one of the stage productions she had called herself acting in. She'd done such a horrible job of it that he'd left just before the curtain closed. To this day, she hadn't heard anything from that guy. "What words of encouragement do you have for me, Ram?"

Steepling his hands in front of his mouth, Ram appeared to be considering his thoughts. He waited a beat, and then said, "Beautiful... I mean, the original singer of that song is certainly pretty, but all I could think about while you held that microphone was how beautiful you are."

"Aww, that's so sweet," Jewel said while giving her husband the eye and nodding in Ramsey's direction as if to say, he should take lessons.

"Sweet, but so fake," Maxine said as she laid Brielle on the church bench and then opened her diaper bag and pulled out the supplies needed to change Brielle. She then squinted her eyes at Ramsey. "That was not the only thing you were thinking while I was up there making a fool of myself trying to sing a song that was way out of my range."

Brielle started making cooing sounds as Maxine smiled at the child while changing her diaper.

"All right, I'll admit it. You weren't that great, but I bet it was still sweet music to God's ears. He doesn't care how well we can sing. God only wants our praise in any way we can give it. At least that's what Mama Carmella tells us. Isn't that right, Dontae?"

Dontae nodded, trying to stay as far away from this conversation as possible.

"Are you all better now that Mommy took that wet diaper off of you?" Maxine asked her fifteen month old as if they were about to start having a conversation.

Brielle cooed and giggled some more. Maxine stood back up and just when she was about to respond to Ramsey's comment, he changed the subject on her.

"Are you hungry?" Ramsey asked. "Because I did promise you dinner after church. Remember?"

"I'm starving. Where are we going?"

"I made reservations at Bentley's on 27."

"Wow," Jewel's mouth hung open for a moment then she said, "You don't mess around, do you, Ram?" She reached out for Brielle; the child went to her with ease. "I guess this means Dontae and I are watching the baby."

"You don't have to do that," Ram told them. "I made reservations for the three of us."

"Please." Jewel waved him off. "Brielle will be just fine with us. She doesn't even have all of her teeth yet, so she can just go home with me and Dontae and eat the mashed potatoes that I cooked."

"Thanks, Jewel," Maxine kissed her sister on the cheek again. She hadn't dated since Brielle came to stay with her, so she hadn't given much thought as to whether or not Brielle should hang out with her on a date, but Jewel was probably right about this one.

Ramsey walked her out of the church. "Are you going to follow me or do you just want to ride in my truck?"

"Let me follow you. That way you won't have to drive all the way back on this side of town to bring me to my car."

"Okay, sounds good. I'll walk you to your car."

"Thanks, Ram, how gentlemanly of you." They took a few steps toward her car, and then Maxine put her arm on his shoulder and stopped walking. "I owe you an apology. I shouldn't have invited you to church today. And I hope you won't hold my flailing talent search against me."

Ramsey put her hand in his and allowed her to lead him to the car. While they walked, he said, "Seems as if it's really important to you."

She nodded. "Ever since giving up modeling, I've been trying to discover what else I'm good at. But I've been a big flop at the things I've tried so far... acting, dancing, singing... you name it."

"I can understand trying to find another career. Not many people retire in their thirties. But maybe you should stick with what you know. If you don't want to model anymore, maybe open a modeling school or become an agent for some of the up and coming models. It's a business that you know, and I'm sure you'd be great at it."

Ramsey was probably right; she needed to stick with what she already knew so much about. But how could she go back to an industry that had cost her so much? "I'll think about it," she said as they crossed the street and headed toward her car.

"Why in the world did you park your car so far away from the church?" Ram was shaking his head as they continued their trek.

"The parking spaces are too close together in the parking lot. I've had my car door scratched a few times, so I'm just trying to avoid acting all hood up in the church, if you know what I mean."

Ramsey's head fell back as he chuckled. But as they approached Maxine's white convertible BMW, the laughter stopped. The hood had been shredded. A piece of paper was lying on the driver's seat. Ramsey leaned over and picked it up, Maxine was too busy screaming into her phone to notice the note.

She was on the phone with the police, asking if someone could come right away. When she hung up, Ram tried to hand her the folded note.

"What's that?"

"It was lying on your seat. Do you want to read it?"

"I can't right now, I'm too busy seeing red. Can you just read it to me, please?" Maxine began pacing around the car. Checking the tires, the paint, looking at everything on the car to ensure nothing but the convertible hood had been damaged.

Ram's eyes got big as he opened the piece of paper.

"What does it say?" Maxine demanded.

"Stay away from my man." Ram read the words off the paper and then he looked up, his eyes questioning her.

But her eyes were full of questions as well. "What man? Who does this maniac want me to stay away from?"

"Now that's something you need to tell me. Because I was under the impression that you weren't seeing anyone and hadn't been for quite a while."

Throwing her hands up, still pacing, she said, "I'm not... I haven't been." Maxine swung around to Ram when something came to mind. "Do you think someone slashed my hood by accident...maybe thinking I was someone else or something?"

"Let's hope that's the case. I'd hate for you and Brielle to be dealing with drama like this over some man who obviously doesn't care what kind of jeopardy he puts you in."

Offended by the way Ramsey readily assumed she had done something to bring this drama upon herself, Maxine put her hands on her hips and let him have it. "Listen up, buddy, because this is the last time I'm going to say this. I'm not dating anyone, and I certainly wouldn't be dating anyone with a psycho girlfriend."

Unfortunately that wasn't the last time Maxine had to make that proclamation, because when the police arrived on the scene, they assumed the same thing. Then when AAA arrived to tow her car to the dealership, Maxine had to once again deal with the same accusations. "For the love of God. I have been celibate for over three years. Now, do I really sound like some kind of temptress who's looking to steal somebody's man?" *Did I really just blurt out my business like that?* But they had made her so mad; she was surprised that she'd restrained herself from saying more.

There was a moment of awkward silence, then the tow truck driver cleared his throat, pointed towards her car and said, "I better get your car hooked up," and walked away.

*Just like a man*, Maxine thought. *The moment one of them realizes that a woman isn't about to fulfill all of their bedroom wishes and dreams they suddenly have better things to do.* She didn't think Ramsey was like that... well, since she'd blurted out her business, only time would tell.

# 6

Ramsey had been knocked off his game by the thought of Maxine being involved with another man. He couldn't believe that he had even imagined marrying this woman and thought it was some sort of sign from God that Maxine would be his wife. He'd been waiting for God to answer his prayer. Now he had to consider that maybe Maxine's slashed convertible top and the note left on her seat might just be God trying to tell him something.

As Ramsey pulled into his driveway, he found himself wondering if Maxine was telling the truth or if she had gotten herself involved in some situation that could potentially bring harm to baby Brielle. He didn't understand how some mothers could be so careless with the children they were supposed to love, while others could simply abort babies as if they were nothing more than non-human fetuses... believing the lies that the world told themselves so they could get away with baby killing.

Ramsey believed with everything in him that God was a forgiving God. A woman who had an abortion was no different from anyone else committing sin. But what could separate sinners is when one person comes to understand the awesome power of God's great love, and His ability to forgive sin. When that person repents of their sins and accepts God's forgiveness, it's like their sin was never committed in the first place. Because if God chooses not to remember a person's sins, who else could be so bold as to cast light on it.

But what about the kind of woman who would kill a man's child without even giving him the opportunity to say whether or not he wanted his own baby? Shouldn't there be a special place in hell for a woman who could rip a man's heart out in a single phone call and then go on about her life as if nothing out of the ordinary had occurred?

Ramsey got out of his car, as he headed into his house trying to get his mind off of his time in New York and the people he no longer cared to remember, he caught a glimpse of a little boy throwing a ball around with his dad. Ramsey had seen the father and son before, but today he stopped in his yard and watched them, all the while wondering if the child Brandi aborted had been a boy or a girl? Was he supposed to be in the yard playing catch or having a tea party with an adorable little girl? He would never know... and that was the one thing about God that Ramsey just couldn't wrap his logical mind around.

If God was so all knowing, why didn't he send Ramsey some sort of sign, telling him to keep his mouth shut and just listen to what Brandi had to tell him that night? He would never know the answer to that question either. And if he asked his stepmother, she would just admonish him to praise God anyhow, even without the answers.

His shoulders slumped as he turned and went into his house. One day he would have a family, and he would treasure them, because he knew firsthand what loss felt like and Ramsey never wanted to feel that way again in life. His stomach grumbled, reminding him that he hadn't had dinner yet. Ramsey went into the kitchen and started making a turkey sandwich. But as he layered his wheat bread with lettuce, tomato and onion, he realized that he didn't want to eat alone tonight. Maxine may have bailed on him, but his brother was always down for a free meal. So he called Ronny and they agreed to meet at Panera Bread on the South West side. Soup and  a sandwich sounded good to Ramsey, just as long as he had some company while he ate it. Plus, he needed to talk to Ronny anyway.

Ramsey had expected to pay for Ronny's meal because his brother put almost every dime he earned back into his business. And after all, Ramsey had cost him funding when he attacked Marlin. But Ronny had already ordered and paid for both their meals by the time Ramsey got there. "I'm the one who asked you to hang out with me. I would have paid for our meals," Ramsey told him as they sat down at their table.

"No need to, bro. You've had a lot going on lately, so I wanted to do something for you."

Ramsey smiled. His brother was a cut up sometimes, but he was truly a good guy. He enjoyed not just being his brother, but also his friend. "Thanks."

"I heard about what happened to Maxine's car. That was crazy, huh?" Ronny dipped his bread in his bean soup while shaking his head over the situation.

"How'd you hear about it?"

"I was at Dontae's house when she picked the baby up."

"Oh." Ramsey took a bite of his turkey sandwich and then said, "But you know what I think is real crazy about the situation? Maxine got mad at me for thinking that she might be seeing someone, since the note in the car said, 'Leave my man alone.'"

"Tough break, especially since you've been trying to get with Maxine for quite a while."

"Tell me about it. I just don't get why she's so upset with me." After having her car towed, Maxine had bailed out on dinner and had just asked him to drop her off at Jewel's house so she could pick up her daughter. Ramsey put his sandwich down. His arms became animated as he asked Ronny, "Wouldn't you assume that she was seeing somebody if some woman shredded her beautiful car's hood over a man?"

Ronny tried to calm his brother. "Yeah, of course, anyone would assume that. Just don't let this eat at you. Maxine will come around."

"I sure hope so. She's the only woman I've even been remotely interested in since I left New York. I felt something for her the first day I saw her... well, actually the second. Because I was introduced to Maxine at the wedding rehearsal, but I hadn't really looked at her, not until she started walking down that aisle." He looked over at his brother. "The thing is, I still feel something for her, but I'll have to get over it if she's caught up in some drama. Because I really don't have time to play games at this point in my life."

"I hear you," Ronny agreed. "But I really don't think that Maxine is like that. All I've ever heard from Jewel and Dawn is how Maxine has devoted herself to her daughter and to finding a new career."

Ramsey smiled, thinking about the choir and the disaster of a cake she'd baked. "And I don't get that either. What's all the urgency about finding a new career? Maxine is in her early thirties and she could easily pass for twenty-four, twenty-five; I'm sure she could still be modeling if she wanted to."

"I don't understand that one either. But just like you had your reasons for wanting to leave New York, I guess she has her reasons, too."

Ramsey nodded, wanting desperately to tell his brother about his reasons. But he couldn't tell Ronny or any of his family for that matter. They all were bible-believing-God's-gonna-fix-it type of Christians, and so was he. But for a time a couple of years ago, Ramsey had lost his way and he didn't ever want his family to know all of that story. So he changed the subject. "I didn't only call you because I needed someone to eat dinner with. I also wanted to talk to you about your business."

Ronny nodded, stirred his spoon around in his soup before answering. "Things are going well. I'm developing a few more products and then my line will be complete."

"How soon do you think you'll be turning a profit?"

Ronny was thoughtful before answering, "At the rate I'm going, I think the business should be profitable in about five years."

Ramsey picked up a napkin, wiped his mouth and then shook his head. "That's too long. I think you could be profitable in a year or two and here's how you're going to do it."

Ronny leaned back in his seat. "I'm all ears."

"I'm going to get you a loan from my bank. And if that won't work, I'll loan you the money myself."

Holding onto the table, Ronny's eyes began to sparkle as he said, "I won't take any of your money, but if you can work out a loan for me, I will be eternally grateful."

They shook on it. "I got you, man. I see how hard you've been working. I just didn't want that little beat down I gave Marlin to stop your progress."

"I was worried at first," Ronny admitted. "But I prayed about it and I decided that if this is the business that God wants to succeed for me then He will make a way. And look at God. I'm in awe of Him sometimes." Ronny was grinning from ear to ear at the thought of the fulfillment of his dreams coming to pass.

Ramsey was smiling, too, but inside he was wondering if he would ever see the awesome power of God in his own life. The brothers parted ways and Ramsey got in his car and headed home, feeling a little better than he had earlier. At least he had done a good deed for the day. Knowing that his brother was happy was all he needed to end his day on a good note.

But as he pulled into his driveway, Ramsey noticed that his front window pane had been completely shattered. "What the devil?"

Ramsey jumped out of his car and ran into the house. Glass was all over his living room floor. *How could this have happened?* he wondered as he walked around the room trying to investigate how his window could have shattered like that. But the mystery didn't last long as he saw two huge rocks lying on his floor.

Ramsey scratched his head as he wondered who in the world would do something like this to him. Ramsey tried his best to treat everyone he met with dignity. So as far as he knew, he didn't have any enemies.

He called Ronny and said, "Man, guess what?"

"What's going on?"

"I just got home and discovered that someone had busted out my front window."

"You're kidding." Ronny's voice held genuine surprise, but then he said, "You don't think Marlin did it, do you?"

"I hadn't even thought of him." Ramsey kicked some of the glass around. "If he did this I might need you to come bail me out of jail."

"Don't go back over that man's house, Ramsey. Just call the police. I'm on my way over. I'll pick up some plastic from Home Depot."

"Thanks, bro. I'll call the police like you suggested. Let them deal with Marlin. I don't want to see him again in life, if I can help it."

They hung up; Ramsey called the police and reported the incident. The dispatcher suggested that he wait for the police outside, just in case a burglar might still be in the house. Ramsey hadn't thought about that. He wasn't interested in being a dead hero, so he left his house and sat in the car to wait for the police.

Ronny arrived just as the police had finished checking the house. "All clear," the officer told him.

"What's going on?" Ronny asked, holding the plastic to cover the window in his hands.

"They were just checking to make sure no one was in the house."

"Good," Ronny said, then asked, "Did you tell them about Marlin?"

"He did," the officer said as he finished jotting a few things on the pad in his hand. He closed his pad and then turned to Ramsey. "We'll speak with Mr. Jones and find out if he was anywhere in your neighborhood today."

"Okay, thanks." Ramsey shook the officer's hand and then went back in his house with Ronny. "Well, let's get started cleaning this mess up. I'll go get the broom and dust pan."

"I'll get the plastic ready."

Ramsey headed to the kitchen to get his supplies. His cell phone rang, but he ignored it because he wasn't in the mood to talk to anyone right then. As he walked back into the living room and started sweeping up the glass, the house phone rang.

"You want me to get that?" Ronny asked.

"No. I don't feel like talking to anyone. Let's just clean this stuff up and then we can chill in front of the TV or something."

But as the voicemail came on a voice that Ramsey hadn't heard in over two years came across the line. All thoughts of relaxing when out the door. "Do I have your attention now?" she asked, then continued as if Ramsey had responded. "Good, so listen up. It's plain and simple, Ramsey, my love. If I can't have you, then you can't have her. I won't allow it."

Ramsey couldn't speak. He was too busy trying to wrap his head around the fact that those were Brandi's words.

Ronny put the plastic down, stared at his brother for a moment, and in his normal way of finding humor in things, he said, "You've got a stalker? Man, when I grow up I want to be just like you."

# 7

The moment Ramsey heard Brandi's voice on his answering machine, he knew he had a problem. And not just any problem, either, but the kind of problem that would slash the convertible top of another woman's car and leave her a note saying, "Leave my man alone." To think that he had practically accused Maxine of carrying on an affair with an attached man, and being careless with the safety of her child. Now that he knew the truth, he felt like the worst kind of judgmental bonehead.

Right after he called the handyman service to have his window fixed, Ramsey ordered two dozen roses and had them sent to Maxine's house with the words, "Forgive Me" on the card. He decided not to call first thing that morning. He had a few meetings to handle first, then he would give her a call after he received confirmation that the flowers were delivered. He needed to tell Maxine about Brandi, but thought a conversation like that would be better received in person.

So he called her after lunch. As soon as Maxine picked up the phone, she said, "Thank you so much for the roses. But you don't need to ask me for forgiveness. I think I was just a little oversensitive yesterday after seeing the hood of my car shredded like that."

He wished he didn't have to ask for forgiveness, wished he'd never had any dealings with his psycho ex-girlfriend. But wishing things didn't make them so. "I was hoping that you had some time tonight. I'd like to stop by so I can talk to you about something."

"I was planning to take Brielle to the park this evening. Do you mind tagging along for that?"

Her voice sounded hopeful. Ramsey prayed that she would continue to sound that way even after he told her that he was responsible for the hood of her car being slashed. "No problem. But how are you getting to the park? Isn't your car still in the shop?"

"It will be in the shop for a couple of weeks. I have a loaner."

"So do you want me to pick you up, or to just meet you at the park?"

"We'll meet you over there. Because if you pick us up, I'd have to switch the car seat and stroller into your car, and it'd just end up being one big hassle."

Grinning, Ramsey couldn't resist a jab. "Motherhood is more than you expected, huh?"

"Way more," Maxine agreed. "But it's also way more rewarding than any of my wildest dreams. I wouldn't trade anything in the world for my little girl."

"That's powerful," Ramsey said, and again, his respect level for Maxine went up. She was some kind of woman. More special than he deserved, but by God's mercy, Ramsey prayed he'd be able to make this work. He jotted down the name of the park and the time she wanted to meet and then hung up the phone and got back to work.

By seven that evening, Ramsey had made his way to the park. He got out of his car and walked over to the sandbox where he and Maxine had agreed to meet. The first glimpse he caught of Maxine took his breath away, the second confirmed what he'd already figured out... he was falling hard for this woman, and really needed her to be okay with what he was about to tell her.

Maxine's hair was pulled back in a ponytail. She was wearing a pair of cut off shorts and a tank top. She was playing in the sandbox like a kid, looking as if she was enjoying every minute of building some sort of deformed structure with Brielle. He wanted to cover those long legs of hers up with sand so he wouldn't have to pray against his wayward thoughts.

To take his mind off of Maxine's legs and the news he was about to hit her with, Ramsey took off his shoes, rolled up his dress pants and climbed into the sandbox with them.

Maxine looked up as he walked toward her. "What are you doing? You're going to ruin your pants."

"I don't care. You two are having so much fun. I can't just sit and watch." Ramsey dropped down on his knees next to Maxine and before he could stop himself, he turned her head toward him and placed a soft kiss on her welcoming lips.

Her eyes beamed up at him. "What was that for?"

"I couldn't help myself," he told her as their eyes locked and held. For a moment Ramsey could believe that it wasn't just him, but Maxine was feeling something for him, too. Brielle waddled over to him and plopped a pile of sand on his pant leg. He took her in his arms. "You want a kiss, too, is that it?" Hugging Brielle to him, Ramsey planted a sloppy kiss on her cheek.

Brielle giggled and then wrapped her arms around Ramsey's neck and hugged him tight. Then the little girl planted a kiss on his cheek.

Ramsey was shocked by how right this felt. He loved being with Maxine and Brielle and couldn't think of anywhere else he'd rather be than in this sandbox with his two girls.

"Looks like you've won her heart," Maxine told him.

Ramsey put his arm around Maxine and pulled her closer to them, he kissed her forehead. "If only the mother was as easy a win as the daughter."

Lifting up on her knees, Maxine whispered in his ears, "You don't have that much further to go with the mother either."

"Is that right?" Ramsey was grinning like a fool in love. He was trying his best to remain cool and not let her peep his hold cards and see that she had already won the game.

"Let's just see how good you are at building castles and then I'll make my decision."

Ramsey lifted Brielle off his lap and got busy with the castle. "Come on, Brielle. We're going to build you a castle fit for the princess that you are." They got busy with the task at hand, joking around and laughing their heads off every time Brielle ruined their sand art. They were easy and right together. Kind of like the feeling of lying on a beach on a warm summer's morning with no pressing business to attend to and nobody wreaking havoc in your life. It felt good like that. And Ramsey wished they could stay the way they were right in that moment. But the castle was built and now, instead of Brielle tearing it down, he would have to do it with the truth of about what had really happened to Maxine's car.

"There." Maxine leaned back and looked at the castle. "We make a pretty good team."

"I hope you continue to think that way."

Maxine glanced up at Ramsey. "I don't like the way you sound. Is something wrong?"

Ramsey picked Brielle up and stood. "I think it's time for us to talk.

Maxine stood up, wiped the sand from her legs and shirt. She also wiped some of the sand off of Brielle and then pointed to a table and bench just past the baby swings. "You want to sit over there?"

He nodded and walked over to the table. Ramsey was more than a little nervous as they sat down across from one another. Everything hinged on that moment. If Maxine thought it was too dangerous being around him because he had a psycho ex-girlfriend, then he would be lost.

Devastated. Destroyed. But he couldn't hide the truth from her.

Ramsey put Maxine's hand in his as he said, "When I got home yesterday after church the window in the front of my house had been shattered."

Maxine's mouth hung opened, then she said, "You're kidding. What happened?"

"I found two big rocks on my living room floor. Ronny came over to help me clean up the mess and I called the police to report the incident, because I thought my sister's ex-boyfriend had done it."

"How is Renee doing?" Maxine's voice held concern in it.

"She'd rather not be at home, but she's adjusting."

"Well, I'm glad she's away from here, especially if her ex is now busting out windows." Maxine shook her head. "That's just crazy."

"It was crazy all right, but Marlin wasn't the one who threw those rocks through my window." Ramsey looked away, took a deep breath and then trod on. "After the police left I received a call from a woman I hadn't heard from in over two years. She said that if she couldn't have me, then you couldn't either."

"What? Why would she be concerned about me?" Maxine's brows were furrowed in confusion.

"I don't know. But here's the thing. I think she slashed the hood of your car."

Maxine stood, took one step then turned back to Ramsey and took Brielle out of his arms and sat back down. "Why would this woman do that? How does she even know who I am?"

"I don't know and I don't know."

Maxine gave him a "yeah, right" stare down.

Ramsey raised a hand as if he was testifying in court. "You've got to believe me, Maxine. I haven't seen or spoken to her in a little over two years."

A little girl who appeared to be about nine or ten years old came up to Maxine and said, "Can I put Brielle on the swings today?"

Smiling at the little girl, Maxine said, "Hey Eboni, where's your mom?"

Eboni pointed over by the slide. "She's with my brothers, but I didn't want to go down the slide all day long." Eboni stretched out the word long to express how longsuffering she had been with her brothers.

"Okay, you can push Brielle. But I'll put her in the swing for you." Maxine got up and walked Brielle over to the swings. "You want to get on these today, Bre-Bre?"

The excitement in Brielle's eyes was evident as she bounced around saying, "Ye... ye... yes!"

Maxine picked Brielle up and put her in the swing. She then turned back to Eboni and said, "Don't swing her too high or too fast, okay?"

"I won't hurt her, Ms. Maxine. I know how to swing a baby."

"Thanks, Eboni. Just bring her back to me when she's ready to get out." With that Maxine headed back to Ramsey; she sat down and glared at him. "So you mean to tell me that the whole while you were accusing me of having an illicit affair with some two-timing man, you were having stalker trouble of your own?"

"It's not like that, Maxine. I never would have called you if I was having trouble with a woman like that. I wouldn't have wanted to bring anything like this to your door." Ramsey was frustrated about the entire situation, because he couldn't figure out how he had gotten himself back on Brandi's radar. He'd done everything he could to get away from her; why was she making an appearance back in his life now? "I promise you that I haven't had any dealings whatsoever with Brandi in more than two years."

Maxine's body jolted as if she'd received a high voltage shock. "Wait a minute," Maxine waved her hand in Ramsey's face. "Are you telling me that your ex-girlfriend's name is Brandi?" Squinting her eyes as if examining him, she asked, "What's her last name?"

"What difference does that make?" Ramsey didn't understand Maxine's reaction. "Do you know someone named Brandi?"

Before Maxine could answer they heard a scream. They both turned and saw Eboni being knocked down and a woman with a hoodie on in ninety-degree weather, pulling Brielle out of the swing. Maxine and Ramsey jumped into action. Ramsey was running like he was doing the fifty-yard dash, while Maxine screamed, "Stop that woman. She's trying to steal my baby!"

A couple of women that were standing in the parking lot connected their arms together, forming a barrier so the woman couldn't get through them. Brielle was crying and the woman was frantically searching for a way around.

She went left and the barrier moved left, she went right and they moved again.

That had been all the time Ramsey needed to catch up to the woman. He grabbed hold of her jacket and attempted to pull her back into the park. "Call the police," he yelled to no one in particular. He reached around and grabbed hold of Brielle. "Let her go," he told the woman. "Your little game is over."

"No," she yelled back. "If you don't want me, you can't have her."

Ramsey was thankful that Maxine had grabbed hold of Brielle at that moment, because when he heard those words and that voice, he almost lost his grip on the baby. "Brandi?"

Ramsey pulled the hood off the woman's head. And as sure as there is a God in heaven, there was also a woman by the name of Brandi Owens who was determined to destroy his life. "What's wrong with you? Why are you trying to steal Maxine's baby?"

Maxine had Brielle in her arms. Fire was just about shooting out of her eyes as she said, "You can't do this, Brandi. We had a deal. You're the one who asked for my help, remember?"

Ramsey turned to Maxine. "You know her?"

Sirens began blaring as the police drove into the park. A few of the other moms were holding onto Brandi and preparing to hand her over to the police when Maxine answered Ramsey. "She's Brielle's birth mom."

And at that moment, with the police taking hold of Brandi, Brielle crying and Maxine looking scared and confused, Ramsey's world changed forever.

# 8

Later at Maxine's house, Ramsey asked, "What did she tell you about Brielle's father?"

"She said he was a deadbeat who left her and the baby."

Those were fighting words as far as Ramsey was concerned. If he would have known about the baby, he would have never left Brandi's side. Maybe they wouldn't have worked as husband and wife, but he would have been there for his daughter. With clenched teeth he said, "She called me a week after I broke things off with her and told me that she'd had an abortion."

"Maybe she did, Ram. Brandi is a very unstable woman. She could have aborted your baby and then gotten pregnant immediately after."

Ramsey acknowledged that, but then said, "The first night I saw Brielle, I saw something in her eyes. Have you noticed that our eyes are shaped the same and we have the same color and everything? Now that I think about it, Brielle and I have pretty much the same skin tone, also. I just hadn't paid it much attention before because I had no reason to, I guess."

"What are you saying, Ram?" Maxine had that nervous look on her face again. The same one she had at the park when she thought Brandi was trying to take her baby away from her.

"I'm saying that I think we need to get a paternity test. If Brielle is mine, I want to know about it."

"And then what?"

He sat down next to Maxine, trying to calm her nerves. "I'm not trying to take Brielle away from you. I can see how much you love her and how much she loves you. But don't you think I have a right to know if I have a child? I've had so many nightmares about Brandi taking her away from me. This would be some kind of miracle, don't you agree... if Brielle did turn out to be mine?"

"She's mine, Ram, don't forget that."

"I know she's yours, Maxine. But please don't take this away from me. Help me to find out if my baby is alive or not."

Maxine crossed her arms. "What if she is yours? Will I then have to fight you and Brandi for her?"

"Brandi has nothing to do with this. She gave Brielle away. But I never gave up my rights to my child, Maxine." Ramsey hated the fear he saw in Maxine's eyes, he hated having to put her through this, but he had to know. "It's like what you told me about feeling as if you put your career ahead of having children and then feeling as if you might have given up the best part of your life. I've felt that way ever since I found out that Brandi aborted my baby...

like I messed up royally, and nothing I did in life would ever fix it. But now I feel like maybe God is giving me a second chance. Don't take that away from me, okay, Maxine?"

With tears in her eyes she said, "All right, Ram, we'll do it your way."

***

After everything that occurred in the last few weeks, Maxine was left wondering what life would be like if she lost Brielle. Brandi had made bail and her lawyer was now claiming that she couldn't have kidnapped her own child and they were challenging the validity of the adoption since the father never signed away his rights.

Ramsey had taken the paternity test and had hired his own attorney. The test hadn't come back yet and even though Ramsey was being so wonderful to her and Brielle, Maxine felt the need to get her attorney involved. She just prayed that she wouldn't have to fight Ramsey if Brielle turned out to be his child. But with each passing day, Maxine was becoming more and more convinced that Ramsey was, in fact, Brielle's father. Her nerves were shot.

Brandi had duped her into believing that she'd had some one night stand with a deadbeat and that Brielle's father would never be in the picture. She should have known not to trust that girl. She had been a flake during the early years of their modeling careers. Actually, Brandi's career ended rather quickly because she couldn't handle the pressure and couldn't keep her appointments. But Maxine had tried to remain friends with her.

They'd lost touch, mainly due to Brandi changing her number. Maxine had assumed that she had left New York. It wasn't until Brandi was eight months pregnant that she'd heard from her old friend again.

"I need your help," Brandi had said.

"Just tell me what you need. If I can help, I'll be happy to." That had been Maxine's response; however, she had no idea that a baby would be involved. But once the idea took root, Maxine couldn't stop thinking about the baby. She decided pretty quickly that she wouldn't let the opportunity pass her by. She retired from modeling with little regret. The industry had taken more than it had given to her, so she knew she wouldn't miss the lifestyle. She willingly left it behind for her child. Maxine just wished she had been thinking with her head and not just her heart the day she picked Brielle up. Letting her emotions lead her, might just cost her the one things she wanted more than anything in this great big old world.

She picked Brielle up and said, "Come on, honey, let's get ready. Your daddy will be here to pick us up soon." She only called Ramsey Brielle's father when they were alone. She wasn't ready to give Ramsey that much power over them yet.

Maxine put on a white sundress and dressed Brielle in a pink and blue jumper set. She put pink and blue box barrettes in Brielle's hair. She packed an overnight bag for her and Brielle and then the two sat waiting for Ramsey. He was taking them to Raleigh to a barbecue at his parents' house. She knew that Ramsey was excited about showing Brielle off to his parents. Maxine just wanted to be able to go and come back home without anyone else trying to take her child away from her.

Her phone rang. Maxine saw that it was Dawn, so she picked up, "Hey girl, I haven't heard from you in a while."

"The real estate market has finally picked up and I have been overloaded with showings," Dawn told her sister. "But I just wanted to check in to see how things were going, or if that psycho woman has tried to contact you."

"I haven't heard from Brandi, but a social worker from Child Protective Services contacted me today."

"Why is Child Protective Services involved? Please don't tell me that Brandi is claiming that you're abusing Brielle?"

"No, it's even worse than that." Maxine's eyes welled up with tears, she wiped them away.

"How could anything be worse than that?"

"I'm not abusing Brielle, so I could defend myself against a case like that. But Brandi's attorney contacted Child Protective Services, telling them that we never finalized the adoption and she wants her baby back."

"What do you mean? I thought you finalized everything when you picked Brielle up from her birth mom."

Maxine had been calling herself all types of fools, but no matter how much she berated herself, nothing would change the truth. "Brandi was real messed up when I arrived at her house to pick up Brielle. She gave me the birth certificate and hospital records and signed the paper I brought with me stating that she had asked me to adopt

Brielle because she was not stable enough to keep her. But we never finalized anything because Brandi went into rehab that day. She promised me that we would take care of everything once she got herself together. But she never got back in touch with me once she left rehab."

"Maxine, you know what this means, don't you?"

"I have a pretty good idea... they're going to take my baby away from me."

"Have you talked to Ramsey about this?"

Ramsey... he was her other issue. "I don't want to tell him, because if it turns out that Brielle is his child, then he will be able to take her from me also. I thought my best hope would be to fight Brandi based on her long history of unstable behavior. But I don't know how to fight Ramsey."

"Why fight him, Maxine? Why not talk to Ramsey and see how the two of you can work together?"

Dawn was probably right. But Maxine had been so full of fear ever since Brandi resurfaced that she didn't know who she could trust. But she didn't have a choice anymore. "I'll talk to him when we get back from Raleigh."

"His parents have an extra bedroom for me and Brielle. Ramsey said he'll sleep on the sofa bed."

Dawn laughed, "As tall as he is, that's going to be one uncomfortable night."

"You think I should take the sofa bed and let him take the spare bed?" At this point Maxine didn't want to do anything that would cause problems between her and Ramsey.

"No, I think you should let that man do for you, whatever he wants. He's a good man, Maxine. And I think he really cares for you. Just open your eyes and stop seeing him as a threat."

The doorbell rang; Maxine took a deep breath and tried to rein in her nerves. "I've got to go, Dawn. I think that's Ramsey at the door."

"Okay, girl. But do me a favor and try to enjoy yourself this weekend."

"I will... promise."

---

Ramsey, Maxine, Dontae and Jewel were relaxing by the pool in Ramsey and Dontae's parents' back yard. Renee, Raven and Carmella were in the house fussing over Brielle, while Ramsey, Sr. and Ronny were grilling.

Ramsey put Maxine's hand in his as he leaned closer to her and said, "I want to tell my family about Brielle after dinner. Is that all right with you?"

"What if I said no?" she whispered, eyes imploring him to understand what she was going through.

"They're going to find out sometime; might as well be now while we're all here together, don't you think?" Ramsey didn't know what he had to do to get Maxine to trust him. He knew how much she loved Brielle and he would never do anything to threaten that relationship.

"What if you're not the father, Ram? I don't think we should tell them until we have proof."

Smiling like a man in the hospital waiting room who'd just been told, 'it's a girl', he said, "The paternity papers came today. I was waiting so I could tell everyone at the same time. But, Maxine, she's mine... one hundred percent."

Maxine popped up, taking her hand out of his. "Why didn't you tell me as soon as you picked us up? What are you trying to do, force me to leave Brielle here with your parents or something?"

Dontae and Jewel sat up, they asked in unison. "What's wrong?"

Dontae and Ronny already knew that he'd taken a paternity test for Brielle. He'd finally broken down and confessed about the reason that he transferred from New York to Charlotte. His brothers hadn't judged him. They had been there for him in the last few weeks, supporting him and keeping his secret. But Ramsey knew that he could hide this thing from his parents no longer. And truth be told, he didn't want to hide Brielle. She was God's gift to him. Even though he had been living in sin when Brielle was conceived, God had preserved his daughter's life and for that Ramsey would forever be grateful.

Maxine pointed an accusing finger at Ramsey. "Ram got his papers back on Brielle and he's just now telling me."

"Calm down, Maxine. It's not a big deal. I had just received my mail only minutes before I picked you and Brielle up. What's got you so on edge? I really wish you would talk to me."

Maxine stood up, grabbed a towel and wrapped it around herself. "What I'm going to do is go back home. I never should have come here with you in the first place.

"I drove you here, Maxine. How do you think you're going to get back to Charlotte without me?"

"I'll catch a cab to the airport," she threw back as she opened the sliding glass doors and stormed into the house. She went into the family room. Raven was bouncing Brielle on her lap. Brielle reached out to Maxine and tears immediately sprang to Maxine's eyes. She grabbed Brielle from Raven and said, "I need to change her."

Carmella followed Maxine out of the room and into the spare bedroom they had put her things in. "Are you okay, Maxine? I thought I saw tears in your eyes."

Laying Brielle on the bed and pulling a diaper out of her bag, Maxine changed Brielle's diaper as she told Carmella, "I'm just not in a good place right now. It probably would have been better for me to stay at home today."

"No it wouldn't have been. I wanted you here today... with me," Ramsey told her as his imposing figure stood in the doorway.

Carmella put her hands on Maxine's shoulder. "I'm going to let you and Ram talk. But if you need me, just come and get me, okay?"

Maxine nodded, she then handed Ramsey the wet diaper she'd just pulled off of Brielle. "Throw that away for me."

Ram threw the diaper in the bathroom trash can and rushed back to Maxine. But she already had Brielle in her arms walking toward the front door. "I'm not going to let you leave like this."

"Try and stop me," she barked at him. "You're keeping secrets and you want me to trust you. No, Ram, it does not work that way. I'm going home."

"Fine, if you want to go home then I'll take you. Just wait here so I can say goodbye to my family."

"I'll be outside," she told him snippily. But as she opened the front door, instead of advancing forward, she backed up as two police officers and a tight lipped woman stood on the porch, getting ready to knock on the door.

"How can we help you?" Ram asked, addressing the police officers.

"We're looking for Maxine Dawson."

"Oh God," were the only words that escaped from Maxine's mouth as she all but crumbled into Ram's arms.

"Is this the baby?" the officer turned to the woman and asked.

Holding Maxine, Ram said, "Will someone please tell me what's going on?" His voice was so loud that several members of his family came to stand in the entryway with him.

Ramsey, Sr. said, "This is my house. And this is my son," he pointed to Ram. "So can you please tell us what you want?"

"We received information that Maxine Dawson had kidnapped a baby belonging to a Ms. Brandi Owens. Child Protective Services is here to collect the baby."

"Over my dead body," Ram shouted. "Maxine is Brielle's mother, and..." while his family looked on, Ram added, "I'm her father."

# 9

"What did he just say?" Renee asked as she turned to look at her family with confusion written all over her face.

Ram turned to his family and said, "Could you all go back in the family room? I will explain everything once Maxine and I straighten this out with the authorities."

Carmella started rounding everybody up. "Okay y'all. Let Ram handle his business." As the others turned to leave the entryway, Carmella added, "We'll be waiting for the three of you in the family room."

Ram appreciated that Carmella said 'the three of you', because that gave him hope, and allowed him to keep the faith that even in this situation with the police and Child Protective Services at the door, his daughter wasn't about to leave his side. "Come in. If you all don't mind, we can talk in the living room and I can show you my paternity paperwork. I think that will clear things up."

Ram walked everyone to the living room. He then grabbed his overnight bag and pulled out the official paperwork that he'd just received earlier that day and handed it to the tight-lipped woman who already appeared bored with the situation.

She read the paperwork, nodded, handed it back to Ramsey and then asked, "So who has custody of the child? You or Ms. Owens?"

"Neither at the moment." Ram pointed to Maxine. "Brielle is Maxine's daughter. She adopted her within a month of her birth."

The woman glanced at Maxine, who was looking as if she'd snuck a cookie out of the cookie jar and then back at Ramsey. "Ms. Dawson was notified earlier today that Child Protective Services of Charlotte would be picking the child up on Monday. Therefore, when we received information about her fleeing the city, we naturally had to change our plans and pick the child up today."

"They didn't tell me that they were picking Brielle up, only that they needed to talk with me."

"But you knew what the issues were, so you never should have left town with the child," the woman said matter-of-factly.

"She left town with me. And since I am Brielle's father, there shouldn't be a problem, right?"

Putting her hands in her lap and utilizing a calm voice, the woman said, "The problem we have is that Ms. Owens never finalized the adoption with Ms. Dawson, so the child cannot remain in her home."

"What are you talking about?" Ramsey looked around the room trying to figure out what had just happened.

"I've been trying to find the best way to tell you," Maxine began. But Ram put a hand on her shoulder.

He turned back to the police officers. "This doesn't make that much of a difference, does it? I'm Brielle's father and I will be marrying Maxine, so whether the adoption was finalized or not, she'll be Brielle's mother anyway."

Ramsey's statement just about caused Maxine's head to fall off her body as she turned toward him.

"I see," the worker said, "And when did all of this come about?"

"What does it matter? Brielle has two responsible adults who love her and want to raise her. You can't seriously be thinking about giving Brielle back to the woman who wanted to abort her." Ramsey was furious. He stood and began pacing the floor as his tirade spilled over. "Brandi Owens is not fit to be Brielle's mother. Any woman who could even conceive of aborting her own child shouldn't be allowed within fifty feet of the child." He stopped pacing, closed his eyes as he ran his hands over his face. Exhaustion was beginning to set in, but he had to keep fighting for Brielle.

"Brandi might not have had the abortion as she told me she'd had, after the fact might I add, but she still didn't want Brielle. If she had, would she have given her to Maxine?"

One of the police officers stood. "Look, we're not interested in pulling your family apart." He turned to the Child Protective Services worker. "How can we remedy this situation so we don't have to take the baby from her father?"

\*\*\*

Ram spent half the night on the phone with his attorney and in the Child Protective Services office. Once he was finally able to get an emergency custody order, he was allowed to leave the office with Brielle.

Back at his parents' house, he was finally ready to sit down and confess all. When he was finished, Carmella walked over to him and gave him a hug. "You have been on my heart for over a year now. The Lord had me praying for you so much, that I could hardly get a prayer in for the others. But I trusted God's direction and now I am so glad that I listened and kept praying. The devil has been trying to attack your mind and make you think that you're not worthy of God's love because of what you did a few years ago. Now I know what to pray for."

"And what, exactly, are you going to be praying on my behalf?" Since the day his father married his stepmother, Ram felt a special bond with her. But he also could feel an anointing when he was around her that he rarely noticed in others. He had to know what she was going to be praying, because then he just might be able to believe it himself.

"I'm praying that you beat that old devil at his own game. Get him out of your head, Ram, don't let him win... know that you are special to God and that His word is true; He has already forgiven you. You don't have to carry these burdens of sin any longer. Jesus took care of all of that on the cross."

"Thank you, Mama Carmella."

Carmella turned toward Maxine and smiled. "And don't you let none of this get you down either. Remember, God sees the beginning and the end. And I've got a feeling that this thing is going to turn out better than either of you could have expected."

Maxine nodded, but didn't speak. It wasn't until the following day when she, Ram and Brielle were on the road heading back to Charlotte that she began to question him. "Am I going to be able to take Brielle home with me?"

"Child Protective Services said that she'll have to come to my house. But you're more than welcome to come home with us. And before you think I'm trying to come on to you, I have four bedrooms in the house."

"If you're not trying to come on to me, why did you tell those police officers that we are getting married?"

He eyed her, trying to figure out where the question was coming from— a place of fear or of longing. He figured it was a mix of both, so he wasn't going to play games with her. "I told them that because I think it's the perfect solution. You're Brielle's mom and I'm her dad. Don't you think Brielle should have both her parents under one roof?"

"What about Brandi?"

Ram's fingers tightened on the steering wheel. "Brandi will never get her hands on my child. She would have probably thrown Brielle in the trash if you hadn't come along."

"I don't think she would have done that. You're not being fair about this, Ram."

"Not being fair?" He slammed his fist onto the steering wheel. "She told me she aborted my baby. I guarantee you that those weren't just idle words. She was thinking about doing it. And if a woman can kill an unborn child, I wouldn't put it past her to kill her own child."

Maxine flinched; every word Ram spoke was cutting her deep. "Do you think that you are the only one worthy of God's forgiveness? Since when did one person's sin become any less or any greater than another's?"

Ram hadn't realized that his words would make Maxine angry. But she had been friends with Brandi once upon a time, maybe Maxine still felt some sort of loyalty to the woman. He put his hands on her shoulders and lightly rubbed her arm as he said, "I don't want to fight with you. If you don't want me to talk about Brandi anymore, I'll let it go. But I don't want her coming in between us, okay?"

Looking out the window, watching the cars go by, Maxine responded, "Brandi could never come between us."

"Just what I wanted to hear." All smiles now, Ramsey got off at the exit towards Maxine's house. "Let's go get a few things for you and Brielle and then go on to my house."

\*\*\*

It wasn't Brandi that Maxine was worried about. It was Ram's hatred for what he'd assumed Brandi had done. Brandi hadn't done it at all, but Ram couldn't seem to get past it. Maxine wondered what he would think of her or how he would treat her when he discovered the truth about her. That she had aborted not one, but two babies, and all so that she could stay at the top of her game. The first time she found out that she was pregnant, her boyfriend had just been killed in a car accident and she'd then received the call she had been waiting five years for. Maxine had the cover of Essence.

Maxine had rationalized as so many of her friends had done back then that she had a once in a lifetime chance to make her move in the fashion industry. She couldn't stop the momentum by getting fat and then going on maternity leave. She had the rest of her life to have children. The second time it happened was two years later when she was modeling for Sports Illustrated, Vogue and other top notch magazines. She was doing runway in London and Paris, what kind of life would her child have with her doing so much traveling?

She'd believed all of the devil's lies back then. But thanks be to God, one day her Lord and Savior made Himself known to her and she hadn't hesitated, she crawled her way back to Jesus and begged Him to forgive her for the part she'd played in selfishly killing her own children. Unlike Ram's unforgiving heart, God had forgiven her and He'd wrapped her in His loving arms and told her, *It will be all right, My child.*

Maxine had believed those words God spoke into her spirit years ago. And she'd begun turning her life around. No longer was she only concerned about her career and making it to the next level and then the next level after that without stopping to consider what others might need from her. She now made time for her sisters in ways she hadn't bothered to before, she certainly made time for Brielle. And God, He was number one on her list.

That's why Maxine couldn't understand why God had softened her heart so towards Ram that she was feeling as if she loved this man. But not one time had Ram mentioned anything about love to her. He only started talking about marriage after he discovered that she didn't have the legal documents to adopt Brielle.

What Ram wanted to do for her and Brielle was wonderful, and Maxine loved him all the more for it. But since Ram didn't love her, Maxine doubted that a marriage between them could survive once he found out the truth about her and that brought great sadness to her. Whenever sadness and guilt of her past tried to overtake Maxine, she turned to the bible. Maxine had the bible in her lap right then as she sat in the comfort of Ram's living room, reading out of Mark the 11th chapter.

"Therefore I say unto you, what things ye desire, when ye pray, believe that ye receive them, and ye shall have them. And when ye stand praying, forgive, if ye have aught against any: that your Father also which is in heaven may forgive you your trespasses. But if ye do not forgive, neither will your Father which is in heaven forgive your trespasses."

Those bible verses ate at Maxine's heart, because she knew that Ramsey was treading on thin ice, by having an unforgiving heart. Ramsey was loving and kind to her and Brielle, but his heart had hardened where Brandi was concerned. Maxine didn't want Ram to still be in love with Brandi or anything like that. But she certainly didn't want him hating the woman and constantly condemning her as if he was Almighty God himself. Because if he continued like this, what would happen when he finally had to face what she had done to her own children? And that day was fast approaching, because Maxine could not conceive of marrying Ram without telling him. If he couldn't deal with it and decided that he no longer wanted to marry her, then she would fight him and Brandi in court for Brielle as she had originally planned to do. But she wasn't going to hold malice in her heart towards Ram or Brandi, no matter the outcome. Her mind was fixed in that regard. God had forgiven her, so she would forgive others, no matter how they trampled on her heart.

Ram walked into the living room, stopped and stared at her for a moment and then said, "Look at you, reading your word like a Proverbs 31 kind of woman. I like that."

"I'm not perfect, Ram. Just because I read the bible doesn't mean that I haven't made mistakes like anyone else."

He sat down next to her and lifted her face so that she was looking directly at him. "Hey, I know that you're not perfect and I don't expect you to be."

"Are you sure about that, Ram? Because I don't want to marry you and suddenly discover that I'm living in a house with a man who hates me, simply because he can't do what God admonishes all of us to do."

"Where is all of this coming from? Have I given you any reason to even suspect that I would be anything but a loving and attentive husband?"

Softly cupping his face in her hands, she told him, "I do believe that you would do your best to treat me like gold. But what I don't know yet is how you would treat me once you discover all my flaws and that's what scares me."

Lifting his hands in an I'm-not-like-that kind of move, Ramsey said, "I don't judge."

"You most certainly do. You've done nothing but judge Brandi from the moment you thought she aborted your baby."

"Am I supposed to play nice with that woman? Maxine, you don't know how I was tormented by the thought of my child being aborted."

"I wonder how much God was tormented by the thought of His son having to go to the cross for all of our sins."

"You're not fighting fair," Ramsey declared.

"Oh really," she said as she stood up and put the bible in Ramsey lap. She pointed to the scriptures she just finished reading and said, "Read this and come talk to me when you can explain to me how it's different."

# 10

"Come to bed," Ramsey, Sr. called out to his wife.

"I'm not through praying. Matter of fact, get down here with me," Carmella told Ramsey. "I don't know what's wrong, but Ram needs us. I feel it, hon. He needs us like never before."

Without another word, Ramsey got on the floor next to Carmella and put his hands in hers. "I'm ready, baby."

They bombarded heaven on Ram's behalf, calling on the name of Jesus, the name above every name. Asking God to look out for Ram, and give him the way out of whatever storm he was in. They prayed for Maxine and Brielle also, because Carmella felt as if a war was being waged and the outcome of this battle would set the tone for everything that would happen for the rest of their lives. "Send Your angels down, Father God. Watch over Ram, Maxine and little Brielle. Lead them and guide them in what they need to do and say. We will forever give You praise, in Jesus' matchless name we pray all of this and we count it done, Amen!"

"I thank God for the discernment that He has given you concerning our grown children," Ramsey said as he and Carmella climbed back in bed.

"And I thank God for you and each and every one of our children. I thank God for not just being our God, but our children's God as well. And I truly believe that each of them will come to know and trust God in the same way that we do."

"Amen to that," Ramsey said and then turned out the light.

"I think we should drive to Charlotte tomorrow."

Ramsey turned back on the light and stared at his wife.

Carmella's explanation was, "I want to see my grand baby again."

"All right, honey, we'll head down there right after church if that will make you feel better. Now let's get some sleep." This time when Ramsey turned off the lights, Carmella snuggled up to him and let sleep take over. But God was trying to tell her something, and she prayed that all would be revealed in good time.

\*\*\*

"I'd rather not call the police to have you thrown out of this room, but you've given me three credit cards with three different names and all of them have been declined. So, I don't know what name you're going by today, but all three of you have to leave this instant."

The desk clerk was holding the door wide open as Brandi glared at him as if it was his fault that she was using stolen credit cards and the jig was up. "You don't have to scream through the hallway, and you don't have to stand there and watch me."

"Just get your stuff and get out of here. I'm trying to be as nice to you as I possibly can. But I'm running out of patience."

Rolling her eyes, Brandi said, "Whatever." She put her suitcase on the bed, and started throwing her clothes, shoes and toiletries into her suitcase. She then fumbled around in her purse, looking for something."

The desk clerk pointed towards the hall. "Come on, you can go through your purse when you get to your car."

She found what she was looking for, put it in her hand, put her purse strap on her shoulder and walked out of the room. Before the desk clerk could move from his spot in front of the door, Brandi turned back toward him, opened her hand so that he could see what she had, and then she tased him. The man instantly fell to the floor, convulsing as if he was having a seizure.

"That's for getting loud with me." She then kept walking to her car as if this was just another day and she'd done nothing wrong. But this wasn't just another day. This was the day that Brandi had decided she was going to get even with any and every one who'd even thought about doing her wrong.

She was so tired of waiting on things to turn around and start going her way. All her life she had run into one obstacle after another. Ramsey and Maxine enjoyed getting in her way, well now she was about to get in their way. Ms. Holier-than-Thou Maxine had moved into Ram's house as if God approved of stuff like that. Well, Brandi needed a place to stay while she figured out how to get her kid back. Since Maxine's house was empty, Brandi figured she'd just stay there. And if anybody showed up, well, they'd be sorry.

***

On Sunday morning Ramsey got out of bed with hope in his heart that this would be the day that Maxine stopped being so stubborn and started taking his marriage proposal seriously. Maxine and Brielle were sleeping in the room next door. It wasn't an ideal situation because Ramsey wanted Maxine in his room, in his bed. He wanted them to make babies together that no court would dare to question their right to parent. But before any of that could happen, Maxine had to stop tripping and marry him.

He'd made a promise to God after things blew up with him and Brandi. Ramsey would never live with another woman unless he was married to her. He would just have to find a way to convince Maxine to marry him, because he was never letting her go. Maxine was the woman God had for him. It all fit. Even the way God orchestrated Maxine becoming the mother of his child before he even knew he had a child on this earth. For this Ramsey would praise the Lord until the day he died. "Thank You for keeping my child alive. Now I just need a little help with Maxine."

He jumped in the shower and then put on his church clothes before leaving his bedroom. Maxine and Brielle were already in the kitchen eating their breakfast of grits and eggs.

"I left you some eggs in the skillet and I can fix you some grits if you want," Maxine said as Ram entered the kitchen.

Ram stopped walking, he got this look on his face as he tried to figure the best way of saying, "No nasty food for me this morning."

"Don't worry," Maxine told him. "The grits are instant and even I can fry an egg."

Ram smiled. "I'd love some." He sat down next to his daughter and took the spoon away from Maxine. "I'll feed her while you make my plate, if that's okay."

"That's fine." Maxine grabbed a bowl out of the cabinet, poured the grits out of a packet into the bowl and then poured some water in the bowl and stirred. "How are we going to decide which church to attend this morning?" she asked as she put the bowl in the microwave.

Brielle's grits were a little watery, so she started making bubbles with each spoonful Ram put in her mouth. He had been denied fifteen months of this. It just didn't seem right that Brandi had been allowed to bail and was now fighting them for custody. Where was the justice in that? Maxine wanted him to forgive and let his angry feelings go, but how could he, when he was daily reminded of how many hours, days, weeks and months he had been deprived of spending time with his beautiful daughter.

"Ram, did you hear me?"

"Huh? His head swiveled around to face Maxine. "Did you say something?"

She handed him his bowl of grits with the eggs on top. "How are we going to decide what church to attend this morning?"

"Oh, that's easy. I attended church with you a couple weeks ago. So, I was thinking that you might want to attend my church today, so we can make the decision on which church we'll be attending after we're married."

She didn't fire back, "I'm not marrying you" this time. So Ram thought this was the perfect time to let his eyes do a little sightseeing. From head to toe, Maxine was total perfection. Even headed to church, she was ever the fashion model, with a champagne colored jacket and skirt on. The skirt had these things that looked like shells, made out of silk fabric all over it. Maxine looked divine and he didn't mind telling her. "I guess I'm going to be the envy of every man in church today when I walk in with you and Brielle."

"You think so, huh?"

Ram grabbed her arm and pulled her close to him. "I know so. Maxine, you are beautiful." He stood up, leaned her against the table and let his mouth say everything that was in his heart.

When they came up for air, she caught her breath before shaking her hands and saying, "Ramsey Thomas, Jr., what am I going to do with you?"

"Marry me," he told her and then held his breath waiting for her answer.

Maxine moved out of his arms. She picked Brielle up and then turned back to Ram. "We can talk about that later. Let's get to church. I'll follow you."

"Why can't we just ride together?"

"Because I have to go back to my house after service. I didn't bring Brielle enough clothes and I've been taking painting lessons, but I left my supplies at the house. I have class on Tuesday night, so I need to try to finish the painting I started a few weeks ago."

"Okay." Ram leaned against the kitchen sink watching her as she put Brielle on the floor and picked up a champagne and gold colored hat and put it on her head. She then took her compact mirror out of her purse and worked the hat on her head until it was in just the right spot.

"Can I ask you something?"

"Can I stop you?" she asked, grinning as she glanced up at him.

He laughed. "Probably not. I just don't understand why you're trying to find a different career when you're obviously suited for the fashion industry."

Maxine's shoulders began to slump. Sorrow etched across her face as she looked at Ram. "Let's just say that I've come to understand just how much I lost by pursuing my dreams of becoming a super model. It wasn't worth it, and I'd rather not have anything else to do with the industry."

He could see that this particular subject was hard for her to talk about, so he let it go. "Well, I guess we need to get going." He grabbed his keys and they headed out of the house.

# 11

*Pastor is on fire today*, Ram thought as he listened to the seasoned minister preach and teach the word of God from Matthew the eighteenth chapter and verse twenty-one.

"Then came Peter to him and said, Lord, how oft shall my brother sin against me, and I forgive him, till seven times? Jesus said unto him, I say not unto thee, until seven times: but, until seventy times seven."

Pastor Morrow stopped reading and looked out at the congregation. "That means you need to be willing to forgive a whole, whole, *whole* bunch of times. It also means that if anybody sins against you this many times, they must be crazy, so you need to go on and forgive them anyhow."

He then bent his head low and began reading again, starting at the twenty-third verse:

"Therefore is the kingdom of heaven likened unto a certain king which would take account of his servants and when he had begun to reckon, one was brought unto him, which owed him ten thousand talents. But forasmuch as he had not to pay, his lord commanded him to be sold, and his wife, and children, and all that he had, and payment to be made.

"The servant therefore fell down and worshipped him, saying, lord, have patience with me and I will pay thee all. Then the lord of that servant was moved with compassion, and loosed him, and forgave him the debt. But the same servant went out, and found one of his fellow servants which owed him a hundred pence: and he laid hands on him and took him by the throat, saying, pay me that thou owest.

"And his fellow servant fell down at his feet and besought him, saying, have patience with me and I will pay thee all. And he would not: but went and cast him into prison, till he should pay the debt. So when his fellow... came and told unto their lord all that was done. Then his lord, after he had called him, said unto him, O thou wicked servant, I forgave thee all that debt, because thou desiredst me: Shouldest not thou have had compassion on thy fellow servant, even as I had pity on thee?

"And his lord was wroth and delivered him to the tormentors till he should pay all that was due unto him. So, likewise shall my heavenly father do also unto you, if ye from your hearts forgive not every one his brother their trespasses."

Pastor Morrow closed his bible and then turned back to his congregation. "Why do you all think I took time out to read almost the whole eighteenth chapter of Matthew?" Without waiting for a response from the congregation,

Pastor Morrow said, "Because many of you need to hear it directly from the bible. I don't want you to think it's for your pastor, your mama, your friends or anyone else. I'm trying to tell you that YOU," he pointed out toward the people, "need to hear it from the word of God. Forgiveness is the key to this salvation walk... And I know it gets hard. Believe me, I know firsthand how people can keep messing with you and messing with you to the point that you wind up feeling like you hate them. But I'm challenging you to forgive... that is, if you want God to forgive all the things you've done."

In the back of the room, angels stood at their posts, watching and waiting for their chance to intervene on behalf of God's people. Arnoth, the warrior angel had been assigned to many great men in the body of Christ. He'd won most of the battles he'd entered into on behalf of the Lord. But he'd lost a few. Arnoth was determined not to lose anyone else to the enemy.

"Do you think it's beginning to sink into his head yet?" Steven asked Arnoth.

"Prayer for Ram has reached heaven, so all we can do now is wait to see if he will accept or reject what God has freely given him."

"I fear that this next part of his journey just may break him."

Arnoth held up his sword, always ready to do battle for the kingdom of God. "Then we will fight the enemy and his minions from here to eternity if we have to. Whatever it takes, Ram will finally know God's perfect will for his life."

The other angels said, "Amen!" as they unsheathed their swords and held them high. The battle was on and Ram had no clue, for the bible tells us that we wrestle not against flesh and blood but against powers and principalities and of spiritual wickedness in high places.

"I like your pastor," Maxine told Ramsey as they walked toward their cars.

Ram took Brielle out of Maxine's arms and hugged the child to him. He looked as if he'd just been exposed to a whole new level in God. A level that he didn't know much about and wasn't sure if he could even hang out with rest of the folks on that level. "He was definitely on fire today. He sure lit me up a few times." He let out an uncomfortable laugh.

"Yeah, I kept feeling you flinch," Maxine joked with him.

"You're laughing, but I'm serious. After that message, I'm ready to go find people that have done something to me, just so I can forgive them." They stopped in front of their cars, and Ram added, "And if I've done anything to you, I'd like to ask for your forgiveness."

Maxine waved the thought away. "You haven't done anything but be kind to me since I met you."

His eyes took on a sorrowful look as he quietly asked, "Then why won't you marry me? Don't you know that I'm in love with you, and I don't want anyone else?"

Those words broke her down. She touched his arm, not caring about the people around them who were busily getting into their cars and driving off. "Do you mean that, Ram? I mean... you've never said anything about love before."

"Well, now that is surely unforgivable." With Brielle clutching his shirt, Ram pulled Maxine into his arms, leaned his head down and let their lips meet in a slow and tantalizing love dance. "How could I have neglected to tell you how much I love and care for you?" The smile was now gone, as he expressed what was on his heart. "I need you in my life, Brielle needs you in hers, and we both love you more than words can say. So, how about it, Maxine? I'll never get tired of asking, even if I have to ask you to marry me a hundred or more times."

Stepping out of his embrace, Maxine said, "All right..."

Before she could get the rest of her sentence out, Ram was jumping for joy.

She pulled on his arm. "Let me finish, Ram."

"Oh, sorry about that. I guess I got a bit carried away. Go on, finish."

"I have something I want to talk to you about. And if you can deal with what I need to tell you, then, yes, I will marry you."

He waved his hand in front of her as if indicating that she had the floor. "Tell me."

Maxine looked around. People were still in the parking lot, either heading to their cars or having conversations just as she and Ram were doing. "Not here. I'll tell you at home."

"I like the way you're calling my place home."

Fumbling around in her purse for the keys, Maxine said, "Let me get on over to my house so I can pick up a few more things for Brielle and my painting supplies and then I'll meet you somewhere for dinner."

Ram shook his head no as he took the keys out of her hand. "You go on home. I'll go over to your house and get everything that you need. I'll even pick up dinner and bring it home. I don't want to wait too much longer for this talk."

"Are you sure you don't mind driving all the way to my house?"

"Not at all. Just let your man handle it. Now which one of these keys goes to your house?"

Maxine took the house key off of her key ring and handed it back to Ram.

"Here, I made myself a list so I wouldn't forget anything. Call me if you can't find something."

He took the paper she handed him, then bent down and kissed her again. Then he put a finger under her chin and lifted her face toward him. "I can't wait to marry you. And I don't want you worrying your pretty little head about anything. There's nothing that you could tell me that will ever change my mind about us."

"I hope that's true, Ram. I really hope it's true," Maxine mumbled to herself as Ram walked around to the passenger side of the car and put Brielle in her car seat.

\*\*\*

Brandi had house squatted before. But at least those people had left plenty of food in the refrigerator. But of course she should have remembered that Maxine was a horrible cook. The girl was probably still eating all of her meals out. But that wasn't such a big deal for Maxine, not with all the money she made during her modeling career. Some people are so lucky, Brandi thought. Maxine always got the best jobs... the most money... the dream life. While I keep getting the shaft.

*Well, times they are a changing*, Brandi thought while putting on a dress she found in Maxine's walk-in closet. Brandi was about to borrow/keep a pair of Maxine's shoes, but all of the shoes were too small. She made do with her own shoes, then grabbed the checkbook that Maxine had lying on the shelf. "Time to go to the grocery store."

\*\*\*

Ramsey went straight upstairs to pick up the things Maxine had listed. He grabbed a duffle that had been laid in the corner of the room she used for painting. He glanced at a couple of the paintings, but he really didn't have time to inspect her work. His mind was on the conversation Maxine wanted to have with him—the one that would determine whether or not she would accept his proposal.

He went into Brielle's room and was suddenly struck by a memory of a perfume he had grown accustomed to smelling. It was like the smell of pomegranates and peaches. He'd only known one other woman to wear that fragrance. Ramsey never liked it, so he hoped that it wasn't Maxine's favorite fragrance, because if it was, he would have to tell her why he absolutely couldn't tolerate the smell of it.

He opened the dresser drawers in Brielle's room and pulled out a few outfits, all the while thinking how much fun it would be to go shopping with his daughter. He took a few of her toys off the dresser and then rushed back downstairs. He was on his way out of the door when he suddenly stopped. He felt as if something was in his way and it wouldn't let him move forward. Then a thought came to him and he went back into the house.

If this had been one of his sisters' homes, he wouldn't have left before checking the windows and doors on the bottom level to make sure the house was secure for them. So he walked around house. All the windows were locked except the kitchen window, and surprisingly enough, the back door was unlocked.

Lifting his head heavenward, Ramsey said, "Thank You, Lord." feeling as if his thought of checking the windows and doors had been Holy Ghost intervention. He left the house and locked the front door, feeling confident that Maxine's house was safe and secure.

The angel that had blocked his way and then whispered in his ear, breathed a sigh of relief and then disappeared.

# 12

Maxine had fed Brielle and then put her down for a nap while she waited for Ramsey to come back home so they could talk. She smiled at the thought of his place being "home". For the longest time, Maxine hadn't felt at home in any house or condo that she'd owned. They had only been a place to lay her head. A place for her to go to when she needed to get away from the hectic demands of her career. The closest she'd come to a home, was the house she'd shared with Brielle.

Now she was wondering if she, Ramsey and Brielle would continue to make Ramsey's house a home after she told him about her greatest shame. Sometimes she wondered how God could forgive someone who had been as selfish as she had been. When Maxine tried to wrap her mind around God's ability to forgive even the worst sinners, she couldn't figure Him out. But she was so grateful that He was not just a forgiver of sins... but a forgiver of *her* sins, each and every one of them.

Maxine wiped the tears from her eyes as her gratitude overtook her. "Lord, please help Ram understand that I am not the same person that I was all those years ago when I aborted my children as if they were nothing more than an inconvenience." The tears kept coming as she whispered, "I'm so sorry. I would take it back if I could, Lord. If I had it to do all over again, I would have left the modeling industry a long time ago, and would have borne my children and been grateful for whatever you provided."

Maxine thought she heard Brielle crying. She reached in her purse and pulled out her iPad, pressed the monitoring system icon and watched as Ram walked out of her front door. Maxine couldn't help it, her belly filled with butterflies at the sight of the man who wanted to marry her and have a family with her. She sighed as she laid the iPad down on the coffee table and went upstairs to check on Brielle.

Brielle was sound asleep. Maxine realized that she could have saved herself a trip up the stairs if had she set up her monitoring system at Ram's house. She rushed back downstairs to call Ram and catch him before he got too far away from the house, so he could go back and get the monitoring equipment. But the doorbell rang, distracting Maxine from her thoughts.

She went to the front door and looked out the window. Ram's parents, along with Renee, were standing on the porch. Maxine opened the door and invited them in.

Ramsey, Sr. gave Maxine a hug as he entered the house. Carmella also gave her a hug, and then said, "I didn't expect to see you. I've been praying for you, though, so I should have known that God was up to something."

"I don't think it's God who's up to something, Carmella. I think it's Ram," Renee said as she closed the door behind herself. "Isn't that right, big brother?" Renee yelled throughout the house.

Maxine held a finger to her lips and pointed upward. "Brielle is sleep. And Ram isn't here right now."

"Then what are you doing here?"

Maxine was a bit offended by Renee's tone, but she reminded herself of how wounded the young woman had been the night she'd seen her in the hospital. She'd overheard the doctor tell the nurse that Renee had lost the baby, so Maxine knew well where her pain had come from. She even understood why she was being so rude now. Renee was operating on that misery-loves-company groove, so Maxine was going to let her slide. "Ramsey has been kind enough to let me stay in the guest room so that I can still be with Brielle while we straighten out this custody thing."

"What's there to straighten out?" Renee asked as if Maxine was the only one confused about something. "The mama gave her away, you don't have adoption papers and Ram is the father. So, naturally, the courts are going to give him custody."

"Renee, that's enough out of you," Ramsey, Sr. said. "We will not stand here and allow you to treat Maxine like this. Now please, find something to occupy your time."

In a huff, Renee went into the family room, flopped down on the couch, and used the remote to turn the television on.

"Please accept our apology," Carmella said, with a mortified expression on her face. "I don't know what gets into her sometimes."

"Nothing for you to apologize for. I know that Renee is hurting right now. I've been praying for her."

"Thank you, we appreciate that," Ramsey, Sr. said.

"Well come on. Why don't we all have a seat in the family room. Ram should be back soon. I just saw him leaving my house about ten minutes ago."

"How'd you manage that?" Carmella asked, curious.

Maxine lifted her iPad off the coffee table, turned it back on and let them all see a shot of her entryway. "That's my house. I have a monitoring system in it so I can check on Brielle. The front area of the house and the kitchen are wired also, just because I'm paranoid." She shrugged her shoulders. "I've read too many stories about nannies beating up on defenseless kids."

"Nothing wrong with a little paranoia. If more people watched over their children like you do, there might be a lot less children walking around wounded. I wish I could have monitored my children's every move when they were younger." Sadness tried to creep into Carmella's eyes, but she shook it off. "I'm going to recommend that system of yours to Joy and Dontae."

"Why wouldn't you recommend it to me?" Renee got up. "You don't think I'll ever have any kids or something?"

Carmella's mouth hung open in shock for a moment. When she gathered herself together she asked, "Why would you think something like that, Renee? I only mentioned Joy and Dontae because they are married. You're not married yet, so I hope to God that you're not thinking about getting pregnant."

Renee's nostrils flared. "There are plenty of single mothers in this world." Renee pointed at Maxine. "Look at Maxine. She's doing it."

Ramsey stood up. "I don't know what's gotten into you, but I wish you would just snap out of it and turn back into the sweet little girl I used to know."

"Calm down, Ramsey." Carmella reached up and grabbed her husband's hand, pulling him back down next to her.

Renee rolled her eyes and then stomped out of the room like a teenager who wasn't getting her way.

Shaking his head, Ramsey looked at Carmella. "We might need to rethink this whole business about letting our grown kids move back in with us."

"Hush, Ramsey. Something is wrong with that girl and you know it. We need to be patient and keep praying. That's it and that's all."

"You can be patient all you want, Carmella, but I'm telling you now, if she talks to you like that again, I'm throwing her out of our house."

"Let me go talk to her," Maxine suggested. Renee headed towards the kitchen when she stormed out of the family room, so Maxine joined the woman in there. She was standing by the sink, holding onto it with her head bowed low. Her body was shaking as if she was crying. Maxine almost turned and left the kitchen. But Renee turned and stared at her.

"Ram told you, didn't he?"

Maxine saw the tears now as they ran down Renee's face. She had been crying for the loss of her own children just before they rang the doorbell, so she felt a connection with Renee. Maxine stepped forward, shaking her head. "Ram didn't tell me, but I know what happened to you. I heard the doctor at the hospital that night." Maxine kept advancing until she was just inches away from Renee. She held out her hand to the young woman. "You're not alone, though. I know the kind of pain you feel. But I also know that God can heal you. I'll pray for you right now if you want me to."

Renee looked as if she was about to give Maxine her hands, but then the front door burst open and Ram came barreling in carrying a couple of bags. "I've got dinner. Is that my dad's car in the driveway?"

Renee wiped the tears from her face and stepped away from Maxine.

"Yes, your parents are in the family room and Renee is in the kitchen with me," Maxine called back. Those butterflies were back. She hadn't even seen him yet, just heard his voice and she was weak in the knees. God help me, she thought. What am I going to do if this man rejects me?

Ram went into the family room and said hello to his parents. He then came into the kitchen and leaned against the door jam, staring at Maxine. "Hey Renee, how's it going?"

He still wasn't looking at his sister, but she answered him anyway, "I'm better."

"Good," he said and then asked Maxine, "So I guess this means our talk is going to be postponed?"

"I think your family needs you right now. Did you bring my supplies?"

He lifted the duffle bag on his shoulder.

"Thanks." She walked over to him. "I think I'll go to a park or something and paint so you can have time with your family."

"Why can't you just stay here and paint?" Ram leaned his forehead against hers.

She wanted to stay. She wanted to be with Ram and Brielle every minute of the day, but things were complicated for them at the moment. Maxine felt it was best just to get out of the way. Besides, she needed to be away from Ram and his family for a while so she could think. She needed to pray and ask God for discernment on how to deal with this man who was offering her love for a lifetime. Maxine only wished she knew what that lifetime would look like once Ram knew the truth about her. Oh she knew she could trust Ram with her heart, but could she trust him with her secrets?

Taking the bag off Ram's shoulder, Maxine told him. "Go check on Brielle. She should be waking up any minute now. I'll be back."

# 13

Brandi was fit to be tied when she arrived back at Maxine's house and found the doors and windows locked. Ticked off and raring for a fight, Brandi went back around to the front door and started pounding on it. If Maxine had come back home and brought Brielle with her, then Brandi had every right to be inside that house. She was sick to her stomach of these starlets who didn't want to actually get all swollen with a baby or experience the agony of birth. No, they wanted someone else to do all of that for them.

Brandi was tired of being used. She was going to show Ram and Maxine just how tired she was. When no one answered the door, Brandi pressed her ear against the door to see if she could hear movement inside the house. But she didn't hear anything. At that point Brandi wondered if she had locked the door by accident.

She glanced around. Maxine lived on a quiet street, but the next door neighbor was always out doing yard work. She didn't want to spook anyone into calling the police, so Brandi figured she would come back once it was dark. That way no one would happen by while she was causing a brick-induced hole in the glass door around back.

Brandi went to a local check cashing place and cashed one of Maxine's checks for two hundred dollars. she then took that money and treated herself to dinner.

***

"You are such a hypocrite, Ram. How dare you preach to me about living with Marlin, when you're over here doing the same thing." Renee glared at her brother as they sparred back and forth.

"I didn't preach to you. And Maxine and I are not living together the way you and Marlin were living together."

"What's the difference? She has her clothes here, right?"

"Yeah, and she and Brielle are sleeping in the bedroom next door to mine. Maxine is not in my bed."

"Will the two of you pipe down?" Carmella came into the kitchen carrying Brielle. "You woke the baby up with all that screaming."

Ram took Brielle out of Carmella's arms. "Sorry about that. I didn't even hear her cry." He turned to Brielle and in his best baby voice said, "Daddy is still a work in progress. I don't hear your cries as well as Mommy does. Do I?"

Brielle was absolutely enchanted with her father. She reached out for his face while blowing bubbles with her spit.

"I love you, too, little one."

"This is the other thing that I don't understand," Renee began. "You know that I just lost my baby. But you brought your baby to our house in Raleigh without even caring how it would affect me. I don't get how you could do that."

Carmella scratched her head as she looked at Renee with confusion written all over her face. "Did you just say that you lost a baby?"

Renee didn't even care anymore. Putting her hands on her hips she turned to Carmella with a smirk on her face. "That's what I said. So you see, if I hadn't gotten into that fight with Marlin, you would probably be getting me that monitoring system for my baby."

Ram watched Carmella, wondering how she was going to react to Renee's revelation. The girl had been an absolute bear to deal with since he'd taken her back home. But Ram saw Renee's anger as a defense mechanism. He was trying his best to be patient with his sister, but his patience was wearing thin.

Carmella walked over to Renee, took the girl in her arms and just held her. Without saying a word, Carmella managed to express love and acceptance for who Renee was and for all she would become in the days ahead.

Renee finally broke and tears streamed down her face. She clung to Carmella as if her life depended on the tightness of her grip. "I miss my baby. I just want to die." Renee cried out.

Ramsey, Sr. stepped into the kitchen, with questions flashing in his eyes. Ram signaled for his dad to follow him. The two men and a baby went into the family room and sat down.

Ram looked at his father for a long moment, then he finally said, "I think Renee is finally ready to talk to you and Carmella about everything that happened to her that night Marlin attacked her. But you might want to prepare yourself, because she's fragile right now and if you say the wrong thing, she might not be able to take it."

"Okay, but tell me what's going on. I'd rather hear it from you, that way when she comes in here, I won't be caught off guard by anything."

Ram nodded. He held his breath for a couple of beats. He then handed Brielle to her grandfather, hoping that Brielle's presence would help his father deal with the next words he had to say. "Renee was pregnant and she lost the baby."

***

Maxine found a park halfway between her house and Ram's house. She took her supplies out and started outlining the trees, but she wasn't finding much inspiration from the green leaf trees. She had begun the painting with thoughts of the trees in her backyard, which were green, yellow, orange and a fiery red. She hadn't been able to recreate the exact look of those trees yet, but she was getting better. Her art professor at the local college where she took classes even said so.

But the trees in this park weren't inspiring her at all. Maxine packed up her supplies and headed home so she could draw the trees in her back yard and then paint with vibrant colors. When she got home, Maxine walked around back. She already had a chair and an easel in the back so that she could come outside and paint whenever the mood struck her without taking the time to set up.

Maxine sat in her chair and drew those leaves and tree trunks for a couple of hours as she just let the time drift by. She knew that she was just avoiding the inevitable, but she couldn't help herself. Ram and Brielle meant everything to her, but Maxine knew in her heart of hearts that she couldn't live with a man who despised her. She was going to have to open her mouth and tell Ram what she had done.

Her cell rang, interrupting her thoughts. Maxine glanced at the call ID. It was Ram. "Missing me already?" she playfully questioned as she put the phone to her ear.

"Already? You've been gone for several hours." He put the phone closer to his mouth and lowered his voice. "When are you coming home, babe? I thought we were going to talk tonight?"

Was she ready to talk? Maybe she needed to quit being such a wimp and just tell him.

"And we've had so much drama going on here tonight that I really need you to come rescue me," Ram told her.

"What happened? Is Brielle okay?"

"Brielle is perfect. Carmella is smothering her with grandmotherly love."

"So where's the drama coming from?" Maxine began packing her painting supplies away as she and Ram talked. She missed him, too. It was time to stop running and face him with her truth. Ram was too good a person not to hear her out and then give her a chance to prove that she was a different person now.

"Renee finally told my parents about losing the baby."

"How did your parents take the news?"

"They were good soldiers about it," Ram said. "Renee is the one I don't understand. Carmella was hugging her and she just kept saying that she wanted to die herself."

"And you don't understand why Renee could feel so strongly about an unborn child?"

"No, I get that. But the way she's acting, it's like she's blaming herself for what Marlin did. Renee didn't run off and have some abortion, like most of these women do, that baby was beaten out of her."

Trying to defend herself and tell part of her story, Maxine said, "Some women who've had abortions might feel as if their babies were beaten out of them also. This world can be so cruel and... and if a woman is weak or vulnerable, she can be caught off guard by people whispering in her ear about her career or about single motherhood, until she feels so beaten down that she—"

"Oh please," Ram cut her off. "Women like that don't care what anyone has to say. I see them on the news all the time harping about how a woman should be able to do whatever she wants with her own body, and no man should be able to tell them it's wrong... not even God."

That had been Maxine's mantra, once upon a time, not so long ago. But then God saved her and gave her a new mind. He also forgave her. But as Maxine sat and listened to Ram, she realized that this man would never be able to forgive or respect her. But whether he knew it or not, women like her did care what others had to say. Right now her heart was breaking over Ram's words. She could feel the tears coming so she quickly said, "Let me talk to you later, Ram. It's getting dark and I need to pack up my supplies."

"Okay, I'll see you in a little bit."

She didn't respond to that, just hung up and lowered her head into her lap and let the tears flow. "Oh God... oh God, if I could take it back, you know I would. But I want to thank You, for forgiving me and for loving me in spite of the things I've done wrong."

As she finished packing up her supply bag, Maxine realized that she didn't want to face Ram that night. She pulled her keys out of her purse and decided that she would spend the night at home and then have it out with Ram in the morning. But as she walked over to her back door and fumbled around for the right key, she remembered that she had let Ram take her house key off of her key chain. At times like these she sorely regretted having only one key for both the front and back door. "Well, maybe God is trying to tell me something," she said to herself as she got back in her car and headed back to Ram's place.

# 14

The first thing Maxine did when she entered Ram's house was to take Brielle in her arms. She hugged the child so tight that Brielle squealed. She and Ram were due in court next week to fight for custody of Brielle. She had a feeling that Ram would be at one table with his attorney and she would be at another with her attorney. Chances of the judge giving her Brielle over Brandi or Ram were very slim, but she had to believe that God could work a miracle on her behalf.

"I missed you so much, Brielle." Maxine trailed kisses all around her daughter's round face.

"Times like this make a grown man wish he was a baby again. Then maybe I could get a little love, huh?" Ram was sitting on the arm of the chair next to Maxine and Brielle.

Maxine looked up at him. "Do you want a bottle, too?" She got up and headed to the kitchen with Brielle. It was time for Brielle's last feeding of the day. Maxine intended to feed Brielle, then put her to bed, and then get her house key from Ram so that she could go home. She didn't belong there, pretending as if they were a family.

As she took the milk out of the fridge and began pouring it into Brielle's bottle, Renee came into the kitchen. She didn't seem as angry as she had been earlier; Maxine smiled at her.

"I've never seen my brother so in love with a woman. What have you done to him?"

Maxine wished she could teach him how not to be so self-righteous... wished she could get him to understand that sometimes otherwise good people do terrible things that they live their whole lives regretting. "I haven't done anything to him."

Renee sat down at the table across from Maxine and Brielle. "Can I feed her that bottle?"

"I think Brielle would like that." Maxine handed Brielle to Renee and then gave her the bottle.

Renee smiled as she looked down on Brielle happily taking her bottle, not knowing anything about the storm brewing around her. "Can I ask you something?" Renee said to Maxine.

"Sure. What do you want to know?"

"Earlier today you told me that you knew how I felt." Renee looked up at her. "Did you lose a baby, too?"

Sighing deeply, Maxine said, "If only it was that simple."

"What do you mean?"

Closing her eyes, she tried to shut out the memory of those days when success at any cost was the only thing that mattered to her and the group of friends she associated with. But Maxine was tired of hiding from the truth. "I didn't lose my babies like you lost yours. I aborted them."

"Woo," was all Renee could say to that news.

"Woo is right," Maxine agreed as her eyes filled with tears again. "I'm ashamed of the way I took the easy way out, and the way I didn't care about what happened to my babies until it was too late."

"That's how I feel," Renee told her, like she was fascinated that they both felt the same way. "I kept telling myself that if I hadn't gotten involved with a monster like Marlin, my baby would still be inside of me. So I guess my shame lies in the men I'm attracted to. There must be something wrong with me, to pick such evil men."

"I've been trying to figure out what's wrong with me that I could have done some of the things that I have done in my lifetime. All I've been able to come up with is that when we don't follow God's path for our lives, we can make some pretty big mistakes... some that we can't take back; we have to live with the consequences forever."

"You sound like you really regret your decision."

Sorrow was imbedded in Maxine's eyes as she said, "I've never regretted anything more." Her body shook as tears spilled out, tears for her unborn children who were not on earth with her. Maxine knew that God had received them in heaven. She had tried for years to let that knowledge be enough for her, but this thing with Ram and Brandi had brought all those memories, and all the guilt back up and Maxine didn't know if she would ever be able to let it go.

Renee took the bottle out of Brielle's mouth and walked around the table to comfort Maxine. "I didn't mean to make you cry. I'm sorry. I shouldn't have pried into your business."

Brielle reached out for Maxine. "Mama."

Wiping the tears from her eyes, Maxine took her daughter into her arms and hugged her tight once more. She looked up at Renee and confessed, "I bought into the whole I-am-woman-and-I-can-do-what-I want-with-my-body movement. But the people who were encouraging me to do what I wanted, forgot to tell me just how guilt ridden the rest of my life would be. They also forgot to tell me just how precious and wonderful it would feel to have a child look at you with complete and utter trust and then call you 'mama'".

Now Renee's eyes were filled with sadness. "I'm still waiting to hear those precious words."

Maxine took Renee's hand and squeezed it. "You will hear those words, Renee. Trust God, and I promise you that the man of your dreams... someone who will be good to you, will find you. And when the two of you do things God's way, I believe you'll find great joy and a whole bunch of babies."

Renee stepped back from that prophesy. "Hold up, I'm not looking for a basketball team. One or two children would be nice. Any more and I just might lose my mind."

"My bad." Maxine had her smile back, enjoying where this conversation was going.

Then Renee said, "I misjudged you, Maxine. And again, I'm sorry for getting in your business."

"Don't worry about it. You just gave me practice for the conversation I came back here to have."

"That sounds like a very long conversation. So before you get into that with Ram, would you mind doing me a favor?"

"What do you need?" Maxine didn't mind putting the inevitable off for another few minutes.

"I was serious about wanting to know more about the monitoring system. One day I will have a baby. And I will protect her just like you are protecting Brielle."

"Sure, come on, let me get my iPad and I'll show you."

\*\*\*

Ram didn't know why he had been compelled to listen in on his sister and Maxine as they talked in the kitchen. But as he heard Maxine admit to having abortions, he felt sick to his stomach. This was the woman he was in love with. Could it be possible that he didn't know her at all?

He wanted to storm into the kitchen and demand that she explain herself. Why had she let him go on and on about women who carelessly have abortions and never once mention that she'd done the same thing? She was trying to play him for a fool, but he would be an even greater fool if he allowed Maxine access to his daughter, because the moment motherhood no longer suited her, she might just bolt, leaving him and Brielle brokenhearted.

But then he heard Maxine cry and say how much she regretted aborting her baby. That surprised Ram, because he had always thought that women who could do such a thing didn't have any room in their heart for regret or to even feel bad about what they had done. But maybe he was wrong, maybe he had been self-righteous about the issue because of what he thought Brandi had done to his child. His mind went back to his pastor's sermon on forgiveness.

Before Ram had time to further ponder the issue, he heard Maxine and Renee walking towards him. He quickly made his way back to the living room and sat down on the sectional with his parents and pretended to be watching the news with them.

Maxine, Brielle and Renee entered the family room. Maxine handed Brielle to Ram and he eyed her as she made her way to the love seat next to Renee. She picked up her iPad and began showing Renee the features of her monitoring system. And Ram was amazed that the two of them seemed like this was any other normal moment of the day and they were just having a casual conversation as if they hadn't just shared the most devastating of secrets.

"And this is the button I push when I want to scan different rooms in the house."

"That's slick," Renee said as she watched the screen.

"Yeah, and you can go from room to room. Check this out." Maxine tapped another link and instead of seeing a view of her entryway, they were now looking at the kitchen. She then hit another link and the camera began panning Brielle's bedroom. As the camera slowly moved throughout the room, Maxine pointed out the white crib that she just loved. "It will convert into a regular bed when she's old enough."

"That was a good idea. I need to remember that," Renee said.

"You need to remember to tell your husband to get a baby bed like that... is that what you meant to say?" Ram asked, challenging his sister to say otherwise.

Renee rolled her eyes. "Of course I want a husband before I have a baby, Ram. I'm just thinking about the future that's all."

Carmella and Ramsey, Sr. breathed a sigh of relief.

But then Maxine pointed at the computer as she said, "Someone is in Brielle's room."

Ram jumped up, still holding Brielle. He looked at the screen and saw exactly what Maxine was seeing. A woman was going through the dresser drawers in Brielle's room. She removed a pair of frilly pink socks and walked over to the bed. One of the girly dresses that Maxine bought Brielle was lying on the bed. The woman put the socks below the dress. She then put a bonnet above the dress as if she were dressing Brielle. "What in the world is going on? I locked those doors before I left your house earlier today."

"I know you did. That's why I couldn't get in the house when I went over there to paint."

Carmella and Ramsey, Sr. came over and watched the scene unfolding, then Carmella said, "We need to call the police."

The woman turned around and Ram saw exactly who it was and said, "No, I need to go over there and handle some business."

"No that woman is not in my house." Maxine was in shock as she watched Brandi sit down in her rocking chair and make herself at home.

Ram snapped his fingers. "I knew I smelled Brandi's perfume when I went into Brielle's room earlier. She's probably been in your house the whole while you've been here. That's why the back door was unlocked when I was there earlier. She probably ran out to get something."

Maxine touched his arm. "Ram, do you realize what this means? If you hadn't locked my back door, I would be there right now and Lord knows what she would have done. She doesn't seem to be in the right state of mind."

Ram was furious. He might not be sure where his and Maxine's relationship was headed, but he knew one thing for sure, he wasn't about to let Brandi harm Maxine. *Brandi's reign of terror is going to end tonight, because I'm going to put a stop to it,* he thought as he grabbed his keys. "I'll be back."

Carmella grabbed hold of him. "What are you going to do, Ram? Go over there and try to beat some sense into that woman like you did with Marlin? You think you can handle this yourself, but we need to give this battle to the Lord."

Ram loved God and he believed in Him. The only problem was, he just didn't understand Him. Why hadn't God stopped Brandi from entering Maxine's house? If he hadn't locked the doors, Maxine would probably still be in that house fighting it out with Brandi. "God doesn't handle all of our problems, Mama Carmella. Sometimes we have to fight our own way out."

"God is a better fighter than you will ever be."

Ram clinched his fists. He was tired of standing by while the people he loved were victimized. He wasn't letting it happen this time. "You all can pray. I'm going over there," Ram handed Brielle back to Maxine and made his way to the door.

Renee picked up the phone. "I'm calling the police."

"You heard him, y'all. Let's pray," Carmella said while she, Ramsey and Maxine touched and agreed.


"He's not ready yet," Steven said to Arnoth as they watched Ram storm out of the house.

"Do you hear that?" Arnoth asked Steven.

"Hear what?"

"The prayers of the saints. They are bombarding heaven on Ram's behalf. He will either get ready tonight, or be stuck where he is, never truly knowing the power he possesses within him as a child of God."

"I guess we have a whole lot of work to do tonight," Steven said, putting a hand on his sword.

"We can do a little, but most of the work is going to come from Ram on this night."

# 15

"Brandi, get down here. You and I are going to have it out once and for all," Ram said as he opened Maxine's front door. He stood at the bottom of the stairs waiting for Brandi to appear.

"I know you can hear me. I'm not playing games with you anymore." Ram was just about to climb the stairs, go pull Brandi out of that rocking chair and drag her out of that house. Ram didn't believe in putting his hands on women, but he would make an exception for Brandi and do his time with a smile on his face, if need be.

As he put his foot on the first step, Brandi appeared at the top of the stairs. She was looking at him like he was her king and she was getting ready to bow down to him. "Baby, you finally came back to me."

"Brandi, have you lost your whole mind? You're in Maxine's house. I came to throw you out of here."

Her hands were behind her back as she descended the stairs. "Maxine doesn't matter. You and Brielle are the only people that matter to me. I messed up with you, Ram. But I'm begging you to forgive me. Give me a chance to show you how good things could be with you, me and Brielle."

"Is this a joke? Do you know what you put me through with all the lies about how you aborted my baby? I missed a whole year of Brielle's life because of your vindictiveness. And now you want me to forgive you and pick up where we left off?"

She was five steps from the bottom. "That's what I want, Ram. I'm begging you to say that you want the same thing."

He laughed in her face. "The best I can do is warn you that the cops are on the way. You might want to get out before you get arrested again."

"All right, Ram, you win. I believe that you don't want me anymore."

"Good." He stretched out his hand toward the front door, and began saying, "Now if you could just—"

Brandi brought her right hand from behind her back and pushed the bottom on the taser she was holding. The first zap sent so much voltage through Ram that he looked as if he was having a seizure. The second voltage knocked him to the ground. He hit his head and was out like a light.

***

Maxine covered her mouth with her hand as her heart dropped to her feet. Ram, the man she loved had just been tased and he looked to be unconscious.

Ramsey, Sr. grabbed his keys and started barking orders. "Come on, we're going over there. Maxine, give Brielle to Renee. She can stay here and call the police again. We need you at the house when the police show up."

Maxine handed Brielle over, and kissed her on the forehead. She then pointed at her iPad and as tears rolled down her face, she instructed Renee, "Keep watching. Tell the police everything you see."

"I will." Renee was crying, too. "Hurry up, get my brother out of that house before that woman kills him."

"He won't die. He can't. I love him too much," Maxine admitted to everyone listening. They left the house. Ramsey drove while Carmella and Maxine sat in the back holding hands and praying for God to intervene.

***

Renee watched in horror as Brandi tied her brother's hands behind his back and then tied his legs together. After that she turned him onto his back and sat on his chest. Brandi slapped him a few times and she heard her screaming at him to wake up. "Where are the police? What's taking so long?" Renee was frantic with worry for her brother. She dialed 911 again.

The 911 operator sounded a little annoyed as she said, "Ma'am, for the third time, officers have already been dispatched to that location. They should already be there."

"Well they aren't," Renee screamed at the woman and then hung up the phone.

*What should I do?* Renee wondered as she paced the floor. The only thing her family had ever taught her to do in times like these was to get down on her knees and pray like someone's life depended on it. She laid Brielle on the sofa, turned off the iPad, because she couldn't keep her eyes on what Brandi was doing. She needed to put her trust in God and believe He was able to see Ram through this situation even without seeing it.

***

"Lord, we need you right now. We need you to send your ministering angels to work this situation out on our behalf. We don't know how it's going to be worked out or what needs to be done to save Ram tonight. We just trust You to do it," Carmella prayed.

"And we thank You, Lord for all that You are working out for Ram tonight. Bring him back to us safely. Thank You, Lord Jesus, thank You," Maxine added.

The car was full of praise, thanksgiving and prayer as Ramsey, Sr. joined his prayers with theirs. They didn't know what their prayers were doing, but they believed that God was listening and that He would respond.

Arnoth, the warrior angel was at that moment receiving extra power from the prayers of the saints. And he was using that power to run the police in circles. Every time they drove up near the house, Arnoth would raise his arms and cause them to see visions of a dirt road.

"What happened to all the houses?" one of the police officers asked his partner.

The other officer took off his glasses and poked his head out the window. "I've been on this street at least a hundred times; I know there was a house right there." He pointed at the spot where Maxine's house was.

"Well, let's just keep looking." The officers drove off and Arnoth put his hands down.

Steven rushed to Arnoth's side and reported. "She's got a knife and there are two demons in there encouraging her to stab him."

"Come on, Ram. Please open your heart to God. Let Him fight this battle for you."

***

"You don't want me anymore, fine," Brandi said with finality in her voice. "But you don't get to have Brielle without me. And I'm not going to be alone while you run off and marry Maxine. That's not going to happen."

As Ram came to, he realized that his hands and feet were tied and that he couldn't defend himself against Brandi if he wanted to. That's when Ram began to understand what Carmella had been trying to tell him about letting God fight his battles.

"I'm serious, Ram. I'm not going to be one of those silly women who kill themselves
because some man fell out of love with them. I'm going to kill you. And then I'm going to kill Maxine and I will take my baby back." She lifted the knife so that he could see that she was serious.

"You don't have to do this, Brandi. If you want us to be together, we can talk about it," he said in her hearing, but inside he was screaming, *Jesus, I need You. Please Lord, fight this battle for me. Help me, Lord. I don't want to die. I want to live and see my daughter grow up and I want to marry Maxine.* When he heard those words rumbling around in his mind, Ram realized at that moment that Maxine's past didn't matter to him. He was lying on the floor hog tied looking up at his past, and it didn't look so good to him. How could he judge Maxine for the mistakes of her past when he had made some whoppers himself?

"You don't mean it, Ram. I know you don't love me."

Ramsey ignored Brandi. He didn't know what was going to happen next, but he figured that what ever it was, it would happen while he was praising God. "Thank You, Lord for always being hear for me. I love You Lord. I thank You that my daughter will grow up happy, healthy and loved... and I thank You for the love I finally found."

"I know you're talking about Maxine. And I will never let you live to love that woman." Brandi came at him with the knife.

Ramsey rolled onto his side and yelled. "Jesus!"

Arnoth, Steven and all of heaven had heard Ram plead with God to fight his battle. They'd heard him call on the name of Jesus in his time of need, rather than try to figure his way out on his own. The police pulled up to the house. And this time, instead of Arnoth hiding the house from them, he ushered them in by sending a soft wind that blew the front door wide open.

When the door flew open, Brandi stood over Ram. She lifted the knife, getting ready to jab it in his stomach. Ram screamed out loud, "Jesus, help me!"

The police officers rushed in and threw Brandi to the floor. As she was being handcuffed, Brandi was shouting, spitting and hollering, "Leave me alone. He doesn't deserve to live."

One of the officers looked at the other and asked, "Did we just interrupt an episode of Snapped or what?"

***

By the time his parents and Maxine arrived on the scene, Ram was standing on the front porch, listening to Brandi rant and rave while being put in the back seat of the police car.

His parents walked over to him. Ramsey, Sr. put a hand on Ram's shoulder. "We saw that woman tase you, son. I tell you what, I've never been so afraid in all my life."

Ram tried to make light of the situation. He couldn't even imagine how much heartache his impetuous decision had caused his parents. So he hunched his shoulders and said, "Who knew Brandi had a taser?"

"That's why it's always best to pray before you enter into uncertain situations," Carmella reminded him.

"You'll get no argument from me on that anymore, because I can tell you that I practically had a revival with just me and Jesus while I was lying on that floor hog tied like that."

"Amen!" Carmella said.

Maxine had been at the bottom of the driveway answering a few questions that the police officers had for her. But the moment they got in their car and backed out of her driveway, she fixed her eyes on Ram. She ran to him with her arms open wide. "Ram, Ram, oh thank God that you're alive." She hugged him just as tight as she had been hugging Brielle earlier. "I don't know what I would have done if we had lost you."

Even though Maxine had not yet said the words, Ram knew in his heart that Maxine loved him. He loved her, also—more than he ever thought possible. And since God had shown him the error of his ways, Ram would not let the past stand in their way. He trusted this woman with not only his life, but Brielle's life as well. With his arms wrapped around her, he said, "I heard what you told Renee, and I want you to know that it doesn't matter to me. I love you and I want you to marry me. What do you say, Maxine. Will you marry me and make me the happiest man on earth?"

Maxine began kissing him like he was the oxygen she needed to breathe. When the kiss ended, she told him, "I will marry you today, tomorrow or any day you choose. I love you so much. You and Brielle have made my life complete. And I thank God for that."

# Epilogue

Maxine's love for him and Brielle and her trust in God had helped to free him from his need to handle every situation on his own. Now, as they lay in front of the fireplace on their honeymoon, Ram was about to free his new bride from the guilt she'd carried for far too long.

"What's in the box?" Maxine asked as she leaned against her husband. She was exhausted from the events of the day, but didn't want to miss a minute of what was to come. They had done it the right way, so tonight would be the first night that they would lay in each other's arms.

"Oh, just something I brought for our little bonfire."

She sat up and gave him a quizzical glance. "A bonfire?"

Ram put the box in between them and opened it.

Maxine started laughing. "What are my ballet shoes doing in here?" She riffled through the box and saw the poster that announced one of the stage plays she had been in, her paint brushes and the sheet music she'd used while taking singing lessons. "Are you trying to make me feel bad about myself on our honeymoon?"

"No baby, I'm trying to help you free yourself from the guilt you've been carrying."

"Excuse me?"

"There's one last thing in the box, Maxine."

"I didn't see anything else."

"Because I have it turned over. You'll see it once we throw all of these things into the fire."

"You hated my cooking, too. Why didn't you have a piece of cake in this box?"

Ram shook a finger in her face. "You don't get off that easy. I've already asked Carmella to teach you how to cook. I plan to enjoy meals at home for many years to come. And on the days that my wife isn't cooking them, I'll cook for the family."

"I like the sound of that." Maxine looked in the box again, she hesitated for a moment.

Ram said, "None of these things define you, honey. You've been running from the thing you love, because you gave up too much in order to have it. But if God forgave you, then that's it. All that's left is for you to forgive yourself."

Maxine leaned over and kissed her husband. She then took a deep breath and threw her ballerina shoes in the fire. The fire sparked as if God Himself was encouraging her to keep it coming. So she threw the poster in the fire next, then the sheets of music and finally the paint brushes. She turned back to Ram and asked, "What's left?"

"Now that all that other stuff is out of the way, I thought you'd be able to see it a little clearer. Look inside the box, Maxine."

She did as he requested and didn't see anything but an empty box at first, but then she saw it. It was a picture of her. She was on the cover of a magazine and she was absolutely glowing.

"I don't get it. Why are you showing me this?"

"Because you loved modeling."

She shook her head. "It cost me too much."

"You're a different person now. You won't make the same mistakes. But you've been looking for your next career move, and I'm here to tell you that it's right here." He pointed at the picture.

"I'm getting too old to model; at the most I only have another one or two years in the business."

"Then what about opening up your own modeling agency? You've learned about the good, the bad and the ugly parts of the industry. You could help other young girls steer clear of some of the things that tripped you up."

Maxine kept looking inside the box, but she hadn't answered him yet.

"What do you say, Maxine, will you forgive yourself so that we can live the rest of our lives happy with who we are?"

She nodded. "Yes, Ram. I think I can do that. But if I'm going to forgive myself, then I need you to forgive yourself for everything that transpired with Brandi and then one day, I'd like you to forgive Brandi also."

"I'll get right on that as soon as you open your modeling agency. But the woman did tase me and then tried to stab me, so I'm hoping that you can understand if I need a little more time with Jesus before I can truly forgive Brandi for all the drama she brought to our lives."

Maxine nodded. "I understand. I just don't want you to forget about that message pastor preached a few months back."

"I haven't forgotten. Seventy times seven, right?"

"Right." Maxine smiled at her husband. Forgiveness was a process. One that they would walk through together. She couldn't wait until the day they were free from the things that tried keep them in bondage. She ran her hand across his face as she said, "Thank you for loving me, Ram."

"I will love you for a lifetime." He took her hands and walked her to the bedroom. "Why don't you go on in and get changed. I'll be in soon. I just need to take care of one last thing."

"Okay, but don't keep me waiting too long." She lightly kissed his lips and then disappeared into the bedroom.

Ram just needed a moment to give praise to the Lord. His family had been waiting for this... the day that Ram would write his first Praise Alert. Well, the wait was over. He opened his email and began to write:

*Hello fam, I'm on my honeymoon with the woman of my dreams, and the knowledge of that reminded me that I needed to take a moment to give God praise. He's a good God. And I thank Him for always being there for me, even when I was too knuckleheaded to see that He was there. I thank the Lord for all the good and the bad that has occurred in my life, because every moment of every day has made me who I am... a man who loves his family, his wife, his child and most of all, God.*

*God is awesome, and I thank Him for all that He has done and even the things that He has yet to do in my life and my wife's life... I give Him praise!*

After sending out his Praise Alert, Ram turned off his computer. He then went into the bedroom and got to know his wife in every way that God allowed a man to know his wife. When they were spent, they rested on the promises of God and that was enough for Maxine and Ram.

The End

### Join my mailing list:
http://vanessamiller.com/events/join-mailing-list/

### Books in the Praise Him Anyhow series
Tears Fall at Night (Book 1 - Praise Him Anyhow Series)

Joy Comes in the Morning (Book 2 - Praise Him Anyhow Series)

A Forever Kind of Love (Book 3 - Praise Him Anyhow Series)

Ramsey's Praise (Book 4 - Praise Him Anyhow Series)

Escape to Love (Book 5 - Praise Him Anyhow Series)

Praise For Christmas (Book 6 - Praise Him Anyhow Series)

His Love Walk (Book 7 - Praise Him Anyhow Series)

Excerpt of Escape to Love
5th book in the
Praise Him Anyhow Series


by


Vanessa Miller

# Prologue

"I won't do it, Marlin. I can't believe you're asking me to do something like this." A year ago, Renee Thomas thought she had met the love of her life, but day by day as other things got in their way, the love they had was steadily dwindling.

"It's not like you haven't done it before. Stop being a prude," Marlin Jones said.

"I can't even believe you're bringing that up. You put something in my drink. I know you did it, Marlin."

"I don't have time to argue with you." He shoved a drink in her face. "Swallow this and let's get this show on the road."

"I can't drink," she told him while touching her belly. "I'm pregnant."

"You're what?!" Marlin stepped back, fixing his mouth as if he'd swallowed something foul as he stared at her. "You can't be serious. You better tell me something quick, because this is not how I do business."

"What business? I thought you and I were in love. Don't people that are in love have children together?"

"You knew I didn't want kids when we got together."

"It's not as if I planned it."

"Whose kid is it?" Marlin demanded.

"What kind of question is that? I haven't cheated on you." Renee couldn't stand the sight of Marlin sometimes. He'd been like a prince to her the first few months, taking her on shopping trips, exotic vacations and moving her into his mansion. She thought he loved her and wanted to be with her forever. But things had changed.

"Don't give me that crap. We both know you've cheated on me."

"And we both know that you're a liar and a fraud. I have the paperwork to prove it, so don't mess with me."

He swung around, stood in front of the window and took a few deep breaths. When he turned back towards her, he put the drink in her face again. "I don't have time for this. Drink up and let's get to it."

She took the drink from him. But instead of swallowing it, she threw it in his face. "I hate you."

Snarling like a wild animal, Marlin lunged at her. Renee's eyes widened in fear as she tried to escape the blows he punished her body with. She cried out for help as he knocked her down in front of the fireplace and began kicking her. "Help me, he's trying to kill my baby. Please help!" she screamed at the top of her lungs, knowing that Marlin had guests downstairs. She prayed that someone would come to her rescue.

"No one's going to help you. Don't you get it? You belong to me and I can do whatever I want to you."

"I'm not a slave. You can't do this to me."

"Who are you to tell me what I can or can't do? You're nothing." He grabbed her face and pulled her close as he said, "Get it through your dumb, thick head. You're nothing but what I tell you to be."

"My daddy didn't raise no dummies and I'm not going to be treated like this." She reached out and dug her nails deep into the hand holding her face.

Marlin snatched his hand back. When he saw the blood dripping down his fingers, he grimaced. "Now I'm going to really mess you up."

Renee desperately scanned the room and caught sight of the poker in front of the fireplace; she started crawling towards it. She wasn't just going to mess Marlin up if she got hold of it, she intended to gut him.

But Marlin saw what she was headed for and grabbed it before she could get to it. He then whipped her with it like she was a runaway slave who'd been brought back home in chains.

With every punishing blow, Renee screamed as if he was killing her, because the pain was just that bad. She tried protecting her stomach, but Marlin had no mercy and was now punching and kicking her again.

She could barely speak from the pain, but with the strength she had left, she begged, "Please stop."

He grabbed hold of her hair and yanked. "Are you as dumb as I think you are?"

She didn't fight it this time, just nodded.

"Say it," he demanded with a slap to her face.

"I'm dumb."

"And you're nothing without me, right?"

"I'm nothing," she agreed.

He left her alone then as he walked out of the room, mumbling about how she would be useless to him that night.

She lay on the floor sliding in and out of consciousness. When she was finally able to move, she crawled over to her cell and called for an ambulance. She hadn't admitted that she'd been beaten. Instead she told them she'd had an accident, because she didn't ever want anyone to know how truly worthless she was.

Other Books by Vanessa Miller
Better for Us
Her Good Thing
Long Time Coming
A Promise of Forever Love
A Love for Tomorrow
Yesterday's Promise
Forgotten
Forgiven
Forsaken
Rain for Christmas (Novella)
Through the Storm
Rain Storm
Latter Rain
Abundant Rain
Former Rain
Anthologies (Editor)
Keeping the Faith
Have A Little Faith
This Far by Faith

EBOOKS
Love Isn't Enough
A Mighty Love
The Blessed One (Blessed and Highly Favored series)
The Wild One (Blessed and Highly Favored Series)

The Preacher's Choice (Blessed and Highly Favored Series)

The Politician's Wife (Blessed and Highly Favored Series)

The Playboy's Redemption (Blessed and Highly Favored Series)

Tears Fall at Night (Praise Him Anyhow Series)

Joy Comes in the Morning (Praise Him Anyhow Series)

A Forever Kind of Love (Praise Him Anyhow Series)

Ramsey's Praise (Praise Him Anyhow Series)

Escape to Love (Praise Him Anyhow Series)

Praise For Christmas (Praise Him Anyhow Series)

His Love Walk (Praise Him Anyhow Series)

Praise Him Anyhow Journal

# About the Author

Vanessa Miller is a best-selling author, playwright, and motivational speaker. She started writing as a child, spending countless hours either reading or writing poetry, short stories, stage plays and novels. Vanessa's creative endeavors took on new meaning in1994 when she became a Christian. Since then, her writing has been centered on themes of redemption, often focusing on characters facing multi-dimensional struggles.

Vanessa's novels have received rave reviews, with several appearing on *Essence Magazine's* Bestseller's List. Miller's work has receiving numerous awards, including "Best Christian Fiction Mahogany Award" and the "Red Rose Award for Excellence in Christian Fiction." Miller graduated from Capital University with a degree in Organizational Communication. She is an ordained minister in her church, explaining, "God has called me to minister to readers and to help them rediscover their place with the Lord."

Vanessa has recently completed the For Your Love series for Kimani Romance and How Sweet the Sound for Abingdon Press, first book in a historical set in the  Gospel era which releases March 2014. Vanessa is currently working on an ebook series of novellas in the Praise Him Anyhow series. She is also working on the My Soul to Keep series for Whitaker House.

Vanessa Miller's website address is: www.vanessamiller.com But you can also stay in touch with Vanessa by joining her mailing list @ http://vanessamiller.com/events/join-mailing-list/ Vanessa can also be reached at these other sites as well:

Join me on Facebook: https://www.facebook.com/groups/77899021863/
Join me on Twitter: https://www.twitter.com/vanessamiller01
Vie my info on Amazon: https://www.amazon.com/author/vanessamiller

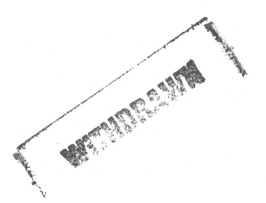

CPSIA information can be obtained at www.ICGtesting.com
Printed in the USA
LVOW04s1511131015

458076LV00014B/454/P

9 781493 574704